# A.B. "Banjo" Paterson's
## HUMOROUS STORIES AND SKETCHES

# A.B. "Banjo" Paterson's
## HUMOROUS STORIES AND SKETCHES

REDWOOD
EDITIONS

## ACKNOWLEDGEMENTS

The cartoons used in this edition all appeared in the *Comic Australian*, a magazine which was first published in October 1911 and ran for eighty-odd issues until June 1913. The Mitchell Library, State Library of New South Wales, has a complete collection from which the cartoons used were photographed.

While every effort has been made to trace the present copyright owners of the cartoonists' work in order to seek their permission, this has proved fruitless in many cases. Angus & Robertson Publishers would be grateful for any assistance in this.

First published in Australia in 1988
by Angus&Robertson
A division of HarperCollins*Publishers* (Australia) Pty Ltd
This edition published in 2000
By Redwood Editions
A division of Hinkler Book Distributors Pty Ltd
17–23 Redwood Drive, Dingley, Victoria 3172, Australia

This edition published by arrangement with HarperCollins*Publishers* Pty Ltd, 25 Ryde Road, Pymble, Sydney NSW 2073, Australia. All rights reserved.

National Library of Australia Cataloguing-in-Publication data:

Paterson, A.B. (Andrew Barton), 1864–1941.
   Humorous stories and sketches of A.B. Paterson.
   ISBN 1 8651 5136 X.
   1. Humorous stories, Australia. I. Title.
A823'.2

Produced in China by Everbest Printing Co Ltd on 100gsm Woodfree

6  5  4  3  2  1
03  02  01  00

# Contents

# Sitting in Judgment

## A SHOW RING SKETCH

THE SCENE is an Australian country show ring — a circular enclosure of about four acres extent — with a spiked batten fence round it, and a listless crowd of back-country settlers hanging around the fence. Back of these there are the sheds for produce, and the machinery sections, where steam threshers and earth scoops are humming, and buzzing, and thundering unnoticed. Crowds of sightseers wander along the cattle stalls and gape at the fat bullocks; side shows are flourishing, a blasé goose is drawing marbles out of a tin canister, and a boxing showman is showing his muscles outside his tent while his partner urges the youth of the district to come in and be thumped for the edification of the audience.

Suddenly a gate opens at the end of the show ring, and horses, cattle, dogs, vehicles, motor cars, and bicyclists crowd into the arena. It is called a general parade, but it might better be described as general chaos.

Trotting horses and ponies, in harness, go whirling round the ring, every horse and every driver fully certain that every eye is fixed on them; the horses — the vainest creatures in the world — arch their necks, and lift their feet up, whizzing past in bewildering succession, till the onlookers get giddy at the constant thud, thud, thud of the hoofs and the rustle of the wheels.

Inside the whirling circle of vehicles, blood stallions are standing on their hind legs, and screaming defiance at all comers; great shaggy-fronted bulls, with dull vindictive eyes, pace along, looking as though they were trying to remember who it was that struck them last. A showground bull always seems to be nursing a grievance.

Mixed up with the stallions and bulls are dogs and donkeys, the dogs being led by attendants, who are apparently selected on the principle that the larger the dog, the smaller the custodian should be, while the donkeys are the only creatures absolutely unmoved by their surroundings, for they sleep peaceably as they walk along, occasionally waking up to utter melodious hoots.

In the centre of the ring a few lady riders, stern-featured women for the most part, are being "judged" by a trembling official, who dares

1

not look any of them in the face, but hurriedly and apologetically examines the horses and saddles, whispers his award to the stewards, and runs at top speed to the official stand, which he reaches in safety just as the award is made known to the competitors.

The defeated ladies immediately begin to "perform," i.e., to ask the universe at large whether anyone ever heard the like of that! But the stewards slip away like shadows, and they are left "performing" to empty benches, so they ride haughtily round the ring, glaring defiance at the spectators.

All the time that the parade is going on, stewards and committee men are wandering about among the competitors trying to find the animals to be judged. The clerk of the ring — a huge man mounted on a small cob — gallops about, roaring out in a voice like a bull: "This way for the fourteen-stone 'acks! Come on, you twelve-'and ponies!" and by degrees various classes get judged, and disperse grumbling. Then the bulls begin to file out with their grievances still unsettled, the lady riders are persuaded to withdraw, and the clerk of the ring sends a sonorous bellow across the ground: "Where's the jumpin' judges?"

From the official stand comes a brisk, dark-faced, wiry little man; he has been a steeple-chase rider and a trainer in his time; long experience of that tricky animal, the horse, has made him reserved and slow to express an opinion; he mounts the table, and produces a notebook; from the bar of the booth comes a large, hairy, red-faced man, a man whose face shows absolute self-content. He is a noted show judge, because he refuses, as a rule, to listen to anybody else's opinion, and when he does listen to it, he scornfully contradicts it, as a matter of course. The third judge is a local squatter, who has never judged before, and is overwhelmed with a sense of his own importance.

They seat themselves on a raised platform in the centre of the ring, and hold consultation. The small dark man produces his notebook.

"I always keep a scale of points," he says. "Give 'em so many points for each fence. Then give 'em so many for make, shape, and quality, and so many for the way they jump."

The fat man looks infinite contempt. "I never want any scale of points," he says. "One look at the 'orses is enough for me. A man that judges by points ain't a judge at all, I reckon. What do you think?" he goes on, turning to the squatter. "Do you use points?"

"Never," says the squatter, firmly; which, as he has never judged before in his life, is not at all surprising.

"Well, we'll each go our own way," says the little man. "I'll keep points. Send 'em in."

"Number one: Conductor!" roars the ring steward in a voice like thunder, and a long-legged grey horse comes trotting into the ring and sidles about uneasily. His rider points him for the first jump, and goes at it at a terrific pace. Nearing the fence the horse makes a wild spring, and clears it by feet, while the crowd yell applause; at the second jump he races right close under the obstable, props dead, and rises in the air with a leap like a goat, while the crowd yell their delight again, and say, "My oath! Ain't he clever?" At the third fence he shifts about uneasily as he comes near it and finally darts at it at an angle, clearing about thirty feet quite unnecessarily, and again the hurricane of cheers breaks out. "Don't he fly 'em?" says one man, waving his hat. At the last fence he makes his spring yards too soon, and, while his forelegs get over all right, his hind legs drop on the rail with a sounding rap, and he leaves a little tuft of hair sticking in the fence.

"I like to see 'em feel their fences," says the fat man. "I had a bay 'orse once, and he felt every fence ever he jumped; shows their confidence."

"I think he'll feel that last one for awhile," says the little dark man. "He hit it pretty hard. What's this now?"

"Number two: Homeward Bound!" And an old solid chestnut horse comes out, and canters up to each jump, clearing them coolly and methodically, always making his spring at the correct distance from the fence. The crowd are not struck by the performance, and the fat man says, "No pace!" but surreptitiously makes two strokes to indicate number two on the cuff of his shirt.

"Number eleven: Spite!" A leggy, weedy chestnut brute, half race-horse, half nondescript, ridden by a terrified amateur, who goes at the fence with a white set face. The horse races up to the fence, and stops dead, among the jeers of the crowd. The rider lets daylight into him with his spurs, and rushes him at the fence again, and this time he gets over.

Round he goes, clouting some fences with his front legs, others with his hind legs. The crowd jeer, but the fat man, from a sheer spirit of opposition, says, "That would be a good horse if he was rode better." And the squatter says, "Yes, he belongs to a young feller just near me. I've seen him jump splendidly out in the bush, over brush fences."

The little dark man says nothing, but makes a note in his book.

"Number twelve: Gaslight!" "Now, you'll see a horse," says the fat man. "I've judged this 'orse in twenty different shows, and gave him first prize every time!"

Gaslight turns out to be a fiddle-headed, heavy-shouldered brute, whose long experience of jumping in shows where they give points for pace, as if the affair were a steeplechase, has taught him to get the business over as quickly as he can. He goes thundering round the ring, pulling double, and standing off his fences in a style that would infallibly bring him to grief if following hounds across roads or through broken timber.

"Now," says the fat man, "that's a 'unter, that is. What I say is, when you come to judge at a show, pick out the 'orse that you would soonest be on if Ned Kelly was after you, and there you have the best 'unter." The little man makes no reply, but makes his usual scrawl in the book, while the squatter hastens to agree with the fat man. "I like to see a bit of pace myself," he ventures to remark.

The fat man sits on him heavily. "You don't call that pace, do you?" he says. "He was only going dead slow."

Various other competitors come in and do their turn round the ring, some propping and bucking over the jumps, others rushing and tearing at their fences, none jumping as a hunter ought to do. Some get themselves into difficulties by changing their feet or misjudging their distance, and are loudly applauded by the crowd for their "cleverness" in getting themselves out of difficulties which, if they had any cleverness, they would not have got into.

A couple of rounds narrow the competitors down to a few, and the task of deciding is then entered upon.

"I have kept a record," says the little man, "of how they jump each fence, and I give them points for style of jumping, and for their make and shape and hunting qualities. The way I bring it out is that Homeward Bound is the best, with Gaslight second."

"Homeward Bound!" says the fat man. "Why, the pace he went wouldn't head a duck. He didn't go as fast as a Chinaman could trot with two baskets of stones. I want to have three of 'em in to have a look at 'em." Here he looks surreptitiously at his cuff, and seeing a note, "No. II," mistakes it for "number eleven," and says: "I want number eleven to go another round."

This order is shouted across the ground, and the leggy, weedy chestnut with the terrified amateur up, comes sidling and snorting out into the ring. The fat man looks at him with scorn.

"What is that fiddle-headed brute doing in the ring?" he says.

"Why," says the ring steward, "you said you wanted him."

"Well," says the fat man, "if I said I wanted him, I *do* want him. Let him go the round."

The terrified amateur goes at the fences with the rashness of despair, and narrowly escapes being clouted off on two occasions. This puts the fat man in a quandary, because, as he has kept no record, he has got all the horses jumbled up in his head, but he has one fixed idea, viz., to give first prize to Gaslight; as to what is to come second he is open to argument. From sheer contrariness he says that number eleven would be "all right if he were rode better", and the squatter agrees. The little man is overruled, and the prizes go — Gaslight, first, Spite, second; Homeward Bound, third.

The crowd hoot loudly as Spite's rider comes round with the second ribbon, and the small boys suggest to the judge in shrill tones that he ought to boil his head. The fat man stalks majestically into the steward's stand, and on being asked how he came to give Spite the second prize, remarks oracularly: "I judge the 'orse; I don't judge the rider."

This silences criticism, and everyone adjourns to have a drink.

Over the flowing bowl the fat man says, "You see, I don't believe in this nonsense about points. I can judge 'em without that."

The scene closes with twenty dissatisfied competitors riding away from the ring, vowing they will never bring another horse there in their lives, and one, the winner, saying:

"Bly me, I knew it would be all right with old Billy judging. 'E *knows* this 'orse."

# Victor
# Second

W E WERE training two horses for the Buckatowndown races. An old grey warrior called Tricolour, whom the station boys insisted on calling "The Trickler", and a mare for the hack race. Station horses don't get trained quite like Carbine: some days we had no time to give them their gallops at all, so they had to gallop twice as far the next day to make up. And one day the boy we had looking after The Trickler fell in with a mob of sharps who told him we didn't know anything about training horses, and that what the horse really wanted was "a twicer", that is to say, a gallop twice round the course. So the boy gave him "a twicer" on his own responsibility, and when we found out about it we gave the boy a twicer with the strap, and he left and took out a summons against us for assault. But somehow or another we managed to get the old horse pretty fit, and trying him against hacks of different descriptions we persuaded ourselves that we had the biggest certainty ever known on a racecourse.

When the horses were galloping in the morning the kangaroo dog Victor used nearly always go down to the course and run round with them. It amused him apparently and didn't hurt anyone, so we used to let him race; in fact, we rather encouraged him because it kept him in good trim to hunt kangaroos. When we were starting the horses away for the meeting, someone said we had better tie up the dog or he would be getting stolen at the races. We called and whistled but he had made himself scarce, and we started off and forgot all about him.

Buckatowndown Races. Red-hot day, everything dusty, everybody drunk and blasphemous. All the betting at Buckatowndown was double-event. You had to win the money first and fight the man for it afterwards. The start for our race, the Town Plate, was delayed for a quarter of an hour, because the starter flatly refused to leave a fight of which he was an interested spectator. Every horse, as he did his preliminary gallop, had a string of dogs after him, and the clerk of the course came full cry after the dogs with a whip. By and by the horses strung across to the start at the far side of the course. They fiddled about for a bit, and then down went the flag and they came sweeping along all bunched up together, one moke holding a nice position on the

THE START AND THE FINISH
He started at 20 to 1
And he came in at Four O'Clock

inside. All of a sudden we heard a wild chorus of imprecations — "Look at that dog!" Our dog had made his appearance and had chipped in with the racehorses and was running right in front of the field. It looked a guinea to a gooseberry that some of them would fall on him. The owners danced and swore in awful style. What did we mean by bringing a something mongrel there to trip up and kill horses that were worth a paddockful of all the horses we had ever owned, or ever would breed or own, even if we lived to be a thousand? We were fairly in it and no mistake. As the field came past the stand the first time we could hear the riders swearing at the dog, and a wild yell of execration arose from the public. He had got right among the ruck by this time, and was racing alongside his friend The Trickler, thoroughly enjoying himself. After passing the stand the pace became very merry, and the dog stretched out all he knew, and when they began to make it too hot for him he cut off corners, and joined at odd intervals, and every time he made a fresh appearance the people in the stand lifted up their voices and "swore cruel" as the boys phrased it. The horses were all at the whip as they turned into the straight, and then old Tricolour and the publican's mare singled out. We could hear the "chop, chop!" of the whips as they came along together, but the mare could suffer it as long as the old fellow could, and she swerved off and he struggled home a winner by a length or so. Just as they settled down to finish the dog dashed up the inside, and passed the post at old Tricolour's girths. The populace took to him with stones, bottles and other missiles, and he had to scratch gravel to save his life. What was the amazement then of the other owners to learn that the judge had placed Tricolour first, Victor second, and the publican's mare third?

The publican tried to argue it out with him. He said you couldn't place a kangaroo dog second in a horserace. The judge said that it was *his* (hiccough) business what he placed, and that those who (hiccough) interfered with him would be sorry for it. Also he expressed the opinion, garnished with a fusillade of curses and hiccoughs, that the publican's mare was no rotten good, and that she was the right sort of mare for a poor man to own, because she would keep him poor. Then the publican called the judge a cow, and the judge being willing, a rip, tear and chew fight ensued, which lasted some time and the judge won. There were fifteen protests lodged against our win, but we didn't have any fear of these going against us — we had laid the stewards a bit to nothing. We got away with our horses at once — didn't wait for the hack race. Every second man we met wanted to run us a mile for £100 aside, and there was a drunken shearer who was spoiling for a fight, and he said he had heard we were "brimming over with — science", and he had ridden forty miles to find whether it was a fact or not. We folded our tents like the Arab and stole away and left the point unsettled. It remains on the annals of Buckatowndown how a kangaroo dog ran second for the Town Plate.

A Series of Sporting Specials, Drawn for "The Comic Australian" by Stuart Allan.
No. 4.—"Fancy Meeting You!"

FANCY MEETING YOU!

# The Oracle at the Races

No TRAM ever goes to Randwick races without him; he is always fat, hairy, and assertive; he is generally one of a party, and he takes the centre of the stage all the time — pays the fares, adjusts the change, chaffs the conductor, crushes the thin, apologetic stranger next him into a pulp, and talks to the whole compartment freely, as if they had asked for his opinion.

He knows all the trainers and owners, apparently — rather, he takes care to give the impression that he does. He slowly and pompously hauls out his race book, and one of his satellites opens the ball by saying, in a deferential way, "What do you like for the 'urdles, Charley?"

The Oracle looks at the book, and breathes heavily; no one else ventures to speak. "Well," he says, at last, "of course there's only one in it — if he's wanted. But that's it — will they spin him? I don't think they will. They's only a lot o' cuddies any'ow."

No one likes to expose his own ignorance by asking which horse he refers to as being able to win; and he goes on to deal out some more wisdom in a loud voice:

"Billy K——— told me" (he probably hardly knows Billy K——— by sight). "Billy K——— told me that that bay 'orse ran the best mile an' a half ever done on Randwick yesterday; but I don't give him a chance, for all that; that's the worst of these trainers. They don't know when their horses are well — half of 'em."

Then a voice comes from behind him. It is the voice of the Thin Man, who is crushed out of sight by the bulk of the Oracle.

"I think," says the Thin Man, "that that horse of Flannery's ought to run well in the Handicap."

The Oracle can't stand this sort of thing at all. He gives a snort, and wheels his bulk half-round, and looks at the speaker. Then he turns back to the compartment full of people, and says, "No 'ope."

The Thin Man makes a last effort. "Well, they backed him last night, anyhow."

"Who backed 'im?" says the Oracle.

"In Tattersall's," says the Thin Man.

# THE COMIC AUSTRALIAN

Registered at the G.P.O. for transmission by Post as a Newspaper.

No. 4, Vol. I.  .EMBER 4, 1911.  Price One Penny.

HOW THE CUP WAS WON.
The Sport (at the psychological moment): "Come on! you Beauty! NOW!"

HOW THE CUP WAS WON.
The sport (at the psychological moment) :
" Come on!  You Beauty!  Now! "

"I'm sure," says the Oracle; and the Thin Man collapses.

On arrival at the course, the Oracle is in great form. Attended by his string of satellites, he plods from stall to stall, staring at the horses. The horses' names are printed in big letters on the stalls, but the Oracle doesn't let that stop his display of knowledge.

"Ere's Blue Fire," he says, stopping at that animal's stall, and swinging his race book. "Good old Blue Fire!" he goes on loudly as a little court of people collect, "Jimmy B____" (mentioning a popular jockey) "told me he couldn't have lost on Saturday week if he had only been ridden different. I had a good stake on him, too, that day. Lor', the races that has been chucked away on this horse. They will not ride him right."

Then a trainer, who is standing by, civilly interposes. "This isn't Blue Fire," he says. "Blue Fire's out walking about. This is a two-year-old filly that's in the stall —"

"Well, I can see that, can't I?" says the Oracle, crushingly. "You don't suppose I thought Blue Fire was a mare, did you?" and he moves off hurriedly, scenting danger.

"I don't know what you thought," mutters the trainer to himself, as the Oracle retires. "Seems to me doubtful whether you have the necessary apparatus for thinking —". But the Oracle goes on his way with undiminished splendour.

"Now, look here, you chaps," he says to his followers at last. "You wait here. I want to go and see a few of the talent, and it don't do to have a crowd with you. There's Jimmy M____ over there now" (pointing to a leading trainer). "I'll get hold of him in a minute. He couldn't tell me anything with so many about. Just you wait here."

Let us now behold the Oracle in search of information. He has at various times unofficially met several trainers — has ridden with them in trams, and has exchanged remarks with them about the weather; but somehow in the saddling paddock they don't seem anxious to give away the good things that their patrons have paid for the preparation of, and he is not by way of getting any tips. He crushes into a crowd that has gathered round the favourite's stall, and overhears one hard faced racing man say to another, "What do you like?" and the other answers, "Well, either this or Royal Scot. I think I'll put a bit on Royal Scot." This is enough for the Oracle. He doesn't know either of the men from Adam, or either of the horses from the great original pachyderm, but the information will do to go on with. He rejoins his followers, and looks very mysterious. "Well, did you hear anything?" they say.

The Oracle talks low and confidentially.

"The crowd that have got the favourite tell me they're not afraid of anything but Royal Scot," he says. "I think we'd better put a bit on both."

"What did the Royal Scot crowd say?" asks an admirer deferentially.

"Oh, they're going to try and win. I saw the stable commissioner, and he told me they were going to put a hundred on him. Of course, you needn't say I told you, 'cause I promised him I wouldn't tell." And the satellites beam with admiration of the Oracle, and think what a privilege it is to go to the races with such a knowing man.

They contribute their mites to a general fund, some putting in a pound, others half a sovereign, and the Oracle takes it into the ring to invest, half on the favourite, and half on Royal Scot. He finds that the favourite is at two to one and Royal Scot at threes, eight to one being given against anything else. As he ploughs through the ring, a whisperer (one of those broken-down followers of the turf who get their living in various mysterious ways, but partly by giving "tips" to backers) pulls his sleeve.

"What are you backing?" he says. "Favourite and Royal Scot," says the Oracle.

"Put a pound on Bendemeer," says the tipster. "It's a certainty. Meet me here if it comes off, and I'll tell you something for the next race. Don't miss it now. Get on quick!"

The Oracle is humble enough before the hanger-on of the turf, and as a bookmaker roars "Ten to one Bendemeer", the Oracle suddenly fishes out a sovereign of his own — and he hasn't money to spare for all his knowingness — and puts it on Bendemeer. His friends' money he puts on the favourite and Royal Scot, as arranged. Then they all go round to watch the race.

The horses are at the post; a distant cluster of crowded animals, with little dots of colour on their backs. Green, blue, yellow, purple, French grey, and old gold; they change about in a bewildering manner, and though the Oracle has a (cheap) pair of glasses, he can't make out where Bendemeer has got to. Royal Scot and the favourite he has lost interest in, and he secretly hopes that they will be left at the post or break their necks; but he does not confide his sentiments to his companions. They're off! The long line of colours across the track becomes a shapeless clump, and then draws out into a long string. "What's that in the front?" yells someone by the rails. "Oh, that thing of Hart's," says someone else. But the Oracle hears them not; he is looking in the mass of colour for a purple cap and grey jacket, with black armbands. He cannot see it anywhere, and the confused and confusing mass swings round the turn into the straight.

Then there is a babel of voices, and suddenly a shout of "Bendemeer! Bendemeer!" and the Oracle, without knowing which is Bendemeer, takes up the cry feverishly. "Bendemeer! Bendemeer!" he yells, waggling his glasses about, trying to see where the animal is.

"Where's Royal Scot, Charley? Where's Royal Scot!" screams one of his friends, in agony. "'Ow's he doin'?"

"No 'ope!" says the Oracle, with fiendish glee. "Bendemeer! Bendemeer!"

The horses are at the Leger stand now, whips are out, and three horses seem to be nearly abreast — in fact, to the Oracle there seem to be a dozen nearly abreast. Then a big chestnut seems to stick his head in front of the others, and a small man at the Oracle's side emits a deafening series of yells right by the Oracle's ear: "Go on, Jimmy! Rub it into him! Belt him! It's a cake-walk! A cake-walk!" and the big chestnut, in a dogged sort of way, seems to stick his body clear of his opponents, and passes the post a winner by a length. The Oracle doesn't know what has won, but fumbles with his book. The number on the saddlecloth catches his eye. No. 7; and he looks hurriedly down the page. No. 7 — Royal Scot. Second is No. 24 — Bendemeer. Favourite nowhere.

Hardly has he realised it, before his friends are cheering and clapping him on the back. "By George, Charley, it takes you to pick 'em." "Come and 'ave a wet?" "You 'ad a quid in, didn't you, Charley?" The Oracle feels very sick at having missed the winner, but he dies game. "Yes, rather; I had a quid on," he says. "And" (here he nerves himself to smile) "I had a saver on the second, too."

His comrades gasp with astonishment. "D'ye'r that, eh? Charley backed first and second. That's pickin' 'em, if you like." They have a wet, and pour fulsome adulation on the Oracle when he collects their money.

After the Oracle has collected the winnings for his friends he meets the Whisperer again.

"It didn't win?" he says to the Whisperer in inquiring tones.

"Didn't win!" says the Whisperer who has determined to brazen the matter out. "How could he win? Did you see the way he was ridden? That horse was stiffened just after I seen you, and he never tried a yard. Did you see the way he was pulled and hauled about at the turn? It'd make a man sick. What was the stipendiary stewards doing, I wonder?"

This fills the Oracle with a new idea. All that he remembers of the race at the turn was a jumble of colours, a kaleidoscope of horses, and of riders hanging out on the horses' necks. But it wouldn't do for the Oracle to admit that he didn't see everything, and didn't know everything; so he plunges in boldly.

"O' course, I saw it," he says. "A blind man could see it. They ought to rub him out."

"Course they ought," says the Whisperer. "But look here, put two quid on Tell-tale; you'll get it all back!"

The Oracle does put on "two quid", and doesn't get it all back. Neither does he see any more of this race than he did of the last one; in fact, he cheers wildly when the wrong horse is coming in; but when the public begins to hoot, he hoots as loudly as anybody — louder if anything — and all the way home in the tram he lays down the law about stiff running, and wants to know what the stipendiaries are doing. If you go into any barber's shop, you can hear him at it, and he flourishes in suburban railway carriages; but he has a tremendous local reputation, having picked the first and second in the handicap, and it would be a bold man who would venture to question the Oracle's knowledge of racing and of all matters relating to it.

# Done for the Double

By Knott Gold
Author of "Flogged for a Furlong",
"Won by a Winker", &c., &c.

## CHAPTER 1
### WANTED, A PONY

ALGERNON DE Montgomery Smythers was a merchant, wealthy beyond the dreams of avarice. Other merchants might dress more lavishly, and wear larger watch chains, but the bank balance is the true test of mercantile superiority, and in a trial of bank balances Algernon de Montgomery Smythers represented Tyson at seven stone. He was unbeatable.

He lived in comfort, not to say luxury. He had champagne for breakfast every morning, and his wife always slept with a pair of diamond earrings worth a small fortune in her ears. It is things like these that show true gentility. All others are shoddy.

Though they had been married many years, the A. de M. Smythers had but one child — a son and heir. He was brought up in the lap of luxury. No Christmas Day was allowed to pass by his doting parents without a gift to young Algy of some trifle worth about £150, less the discount for cash. He had six playrooms, all filled with the most expensive toys and ingenious mechanical devices. He had a phonograph that could hail a ship out at the South Head, and a mechanical parrot that sang "The Wearing of the Green". And still he was not happy.

Sometimes, in spite of the vigilance of his four nurses and six undernurses, he would escape into the street, and run about with the little boys that he met there. One day he gave one of them a sovereign for a locust. Certainly the locust was a "double-drummer", and could deafen the German Band when shaken up judiciously; still, it was dear at the price of a sovereign.

It is ever thus.

What we have we do not value, and what other people have we are not strong enough to take from them.

Such is life.

Christmas was approaching, and the question of what should be given to Algy as a present agitated the bosom of his parents. He had nearly everything a child would want; but one morning a bright inspiration struck Algy's father. Algy should have a pony.

With Mr Smythers to think was to act. He was not a man who believed in allowing grass to grow under his feet. His motto was, "Up and be doing — somebody". So he put an advertisement in the paper that same day.

"Wanted, a boy's pony. Must be guaranteed sound, strong, handsome, intelligent. Used to trains, trams, motors, fire engines, and motor buses. Any failure in above respects will disqualify. Certificate of birth required as well as references from last place, when calling. Price no object."

## CHAPTER II
## BLINKY BILL'S SACRIFICE

Down in the poverty-stricken portions of the city lived Blinky Bill the horse dealer.

His yard was surrounded by loose boxes made of any old timber, galvanized iron, sheets of roofing felt, and bark that he could gather together. He kept all sorts of horses, except good sorts. There were harness horses that wouldn't pull, and saddle horses that wouldn't go — or, if they went, used to fall down; nearly every animal about the place had something the matter with it.

He kept racing ponies, and when the bailiff dropped in, for the rent, as he did every two or three weeks, Bill and the bailiff would go out together, and "have a punt" on some of Bill's ponies, or on somebody else's ponies — the latter for choice. But the periodical punts and occasional sales of horses would not keep the wolf from the door. Ponies keep on eating whether they are winning or not and Blinky Bill had got down to the very last pitch of desperation when he saw the advertisement mentioned at the end of the last chapter.

It was like a ray of hope to him. At once there flashed upon him what he must do.

He must make a great sacrifice; he must sell Sausage II.

What, the reader will ask, was Sausage II? Alas, that such a great notability should be anywhere unknown!

Sausage II was the greatest 13.2 pony of the day. Time and again he had gone out to race when, to use William's own words, it was a blue duck for Bill's chance of keeping afloat unless the pony won; and every time did the gallant race pony pull his owner through. Bill owed more to Sausage II than he owed to any of his creditors.

Brought up as a pet, the little animal was absolutely trustworthy. He would carry a lady or a child, or pull a sulky; in fact, it was quite a common thing for Blinky Bill to drive him in a sulky to a country meeting and look about him for a likely "mark"; if he could find a fleet youth with a reputedly fast pony, Bill would offer to "pull the little cuddy out of the sulky and run yer for a fiver". Sometimes he got beaten but, as he never paid, that didn't matter. He did not believe in fighting, except under desperate circumstances, but he would always sooner fight than pay.

But all these devices had left him on his uppers in the end. He had no feed for his ponies, and no money to buy feed; the corn merchant had written his account off as bad, and had no desire to make it worse. Under the circumstances, what was he to do? Sausage II must be sold.

With heavy heart Bill led the pony down to be inspected. He saw Mr Algernon de Montgomery Smythers and measured him with his eye. He saw it would be no use to talk about racing to him, so he went on the other tack.

He told him that the pony belonged to a Methodist clergyman, who used to drive him in a "shay". There are no shays in this country; but Bill had read the word somewhere, and thought it sounded respectable. "Yus, sir," he said, "'e goes lovely in a shay," and he was just starting off at twenty words a second, when he was stopped.

Mr A. de M. Smythers was brusque with his inferiors, and in this he made a mistake. Instead of listening to all that Blinky Bill said, and disbelieving it at his leisure, he stopped his talk.

"If you want to sell this pony, dry up," he said. "I don't believe a word you say, and it only worries me to hear you lying."

Fatal mistake! You should never stop a horse dealer's talk. And call him anything you like, but never say you doubt his word.

Both these things Mr Smythers did; and though he bought the pony at a high price, yet the insult sank deep into the heart of Blinky Bill.

As the capitalist departed leading the pony, Blinky Bill muttered to himself, "Ha! ha! Little does he know that he is leading Sausage II, the greatest thirteen-two pony of the century. Let him beware how he gets alongside anything. That's all! Blinky Bill may yet be revenged!"

We shall see.

## CHAPTER III
### EXIT ALGY

Christmas Day came. Algy's father gave orders to have the pony saddled, and led round to the front door. Algy's mother, a lady of forty summers, spent the morning superintending the dinner. Dinner was the principal event in the day with her. Alas, poor lady! Everything she ate agreed with her, and she got fatter and fatter and fatter.

The cold world never fully appreciates the struggles of those who are fat — the efforts at starvation, the detested exercise, the long, miserable walks. Well has one of our greatest poets written, "Take up the fat man's burden". But we digress.

When Algy saw the pony he shouted with delight, and in half a minute was riding him up and down the front drive. Then he asked for leave to go out in the street, and that was where the trouble began.

Up and down the street the pony cantered, as quietly as possible, till suddenly round a corner came two butcher boys racing their horses.

With a clatter of clumsy hoofs they thundered past. In half a second there was a rattle, and a sort of comet-like rush through the air. Sausage II was off after them with his precious burden. The family dog tried to keep up with him, and succeeded in keeping ahead for about three strides. Then, like the wolves that pursued Mazeppa, he was left yelping far behind. Through Surry Hills and Redfern swept the flying pony, his rider lying out on his neck in Tod Sloan fashion, while the ground seemed to race beneath him. The events of the way were just one hopeless blur till the pony ran straight as an arrow into the yard of his late owner, Blinky Bill.

## CHAPTER IV
### RUNNING THE RULE

As soon as Blinky Bill recognised his visitor, he was delighted. "You here," he said, "Ha, ha, revenge is mine! I'll get a tidy reward for taking you back, my young shaver." Then from the unresisting child he took a gold watch and three sovereigns, which he had in his pocket. These he said he would put in a safe place for him, till he was going home again. He expected to get at least a tenner ready money for bringing the child back, and hoped that he might be allowed to keep the watch into the bargain. With a light heart he went down town with Algy's watch and sovereigns in his pocket. He did not return till daylight, when he awoke his wife with bad news.

"Can't give the boy up," he said. "I moskenoed his block and tackle, and blued it in the school," meaning that he had pawned the boy's watch and chain, and had lost the proceeds at pitch and toss. "Nothing for it but to move," he said, "and take the kid with us."

So move they did.

The reader can imagine with what frantic anxiety the father and mother of little Algy sought for their lost one. They put the matter into the hands of the detective police, and waited for the Sherlock Holmeses of the force to get in their fine work. They heard nothing.

Years rolled on, and the mysterious disappearance of little Algy was never solved. The horse dealer's revenge was complete. The boy's mother consulted a clairvoyant, who said, "What went by the ponies, will come by the ponies"; and with that they had to remain satisfied.

## CHAPTER V
### THE TRICKS OF THE TURF

It was a race day at Pulling'em Park, and the ponies were doing their usual performances. Among the throng the heaviest punter is a fat lady with diamond earrings. Does the reader recognise her? It is little Algy's mother. Her husband is dead, leaving her the whole of his colossal

ONE PENNY.

# THE COMIC AUSTRALIAN

Registered at the G.P.O. for transmission by Post as a Newspaper.

## A JOURNAL OF FACT, FUN, AND FICTION.

Vol. 2, No. 48.　　　　AUGUST 27, 1912.　　　　Price, One Penny.

1.—"Hold your horse, sir?"

2—"Whoa—a—a!"

3.—"Na—then!"

4.—"Here he is, sir!"

fortune, and, having developed a taste for gambling, she is now engaged in "doing it on the ponies". She is one of the biggest bettors in the game.

When women take to betting they are worse than men.

But it is not for betting alone that she attends the meetings. She remembers the clairvoyant's "What went by the ponies will come by the ponies." And always she searches in the ranks of the talent for her lost Algy.

Here comes another of our *dramatis personae* — Blinky Bill, prosperous once more. He has got a string of ponies and punters together. The first are not much use to a man without the second; but, in spite of all temptations Bill has always declined to number among his punters the mother of the child he stole. But the poor lady regularly punts on his ponies, and just as regularly is "sent up" — in other words, loses her money.

Today she has backed Blinky's pair, Nostrils and Tin Can, for the double. Nostrils has won his race, and Tin Can, if on the job, can win the second half of the double. Is he on the job? The prices are lengthening against him, and the poor lady recognises that once more she is "in the cart".

Just then she meets Tin Can's jockey, Dodger Smith, face to face. A piercing scream rends the atmosphere, as if a thousand school children drew a thousand slate pencils down a thousand slates simultaneously. "Me cheild! Me cheild! Me long-lost Algy!"

It did not take long to convince Algy that he would be better off as son to a wealthy lady than as a jockey subject to the fiendish caprices of Blinky Bill.

"All right, mother," he said. "Put all you can raise on Tin Can. I'm going to send Blinky up. It's time I had a cut on me own, anyway."

The horses went to the post. Tons of money were at the last moment hurled on to Tin Can. The books, knowing he was "dead", responded gamely, and wrote his name till their wrists gave out. Blinky Bill had a half-share in all the bookies' winnings, so he chuckled grimly as he went to the rails to watch the race.

They're off. And what is this that flashes to the front, while the howls of the bookies rise like the yelping of fiends in torment? It is Dodger Smith on Tin Can, and from the grandstand there is a shrill feminine yell of triumph as the gallant pony sails past the post.

The bookies thought that Blinky Bill had sold them, and they discarded him for ever. He is now a bottle-oh!

Algy and his mother were united, and backed horses together happily ever after; and sometimes out in the back yard of their palatial mansion they hand the empty bottles, free of charge, to a poor old broken-down bottle-oh. It is Blinky Bill. Thus has his revenge recoiled upon himself.

A Series of Racing Specials, **Drawn for** "The Comic Australian" by Stuart Allan.
No. 3.—**Bringing** in the Favorite.

**BRINGING IN THE FAVOURITE**
Interfering Wowser Person: "Ah, yes; butchered to make a Roman holiday."
Disgusted Punting Owner: "Well, if you think that losin' your brass is a holiday, this 'ere's
going to be the bloomin' long vacation."

# A Day's Racing in France

THE AMERICAN whose acquaintance I had made coming down the China coast was a very good fellow, but long residence among the Chinese had made him look upon all foreigners as so much dirt, so when we landed at Marseilles he insisted on talking to the French in Chinese "pidgin English", and wanted to beat them when they did not understand him. I can speak French — or at least I used to think I could till I went to France — and I had to do the translating, punctuated with remarks such as "Can do", "Maskee you", "You take luggage topside" addressed by the American to the gesticulating Frenchmen. He was very pleased with himself when he got the guard of the tram to change a 5-franc piece for him, by his own unaided vocabulary, but he got very silent and broody when he found that the money which the guard gave him was all bad. We went to the hotel where most English people go — the same hotel at which there was nearly a riot on the day of Kruger's landing. It seems that, as Kruger's procession passed, some English people who were staying in the hotel threw pennies among the crowd. Now, in France, to throw coppers to any performance is the most deadly insult; instead of hissing a music hall singer who does not please them they throw coppers on the stage — thereby expressing their valuation of the performance. As Kruger's procession passed, a whole shower of coppers was thrown from this hotel. Perhaps the people who threw them did not know what they were doing; on the other hand, perhaps they did! Anyhow, the mob broke out into uncontrollable fury, and besieged the hotel for two hours, while the English visitors cowered inside, and the P. & O. boat had to delay her departure for a long time before the passengers could get down to the wharf. But, when the American and I arrived, all the excitement and frenzy had subsided, and beyond the fact that they looked upon all English-speaking people as assassins, they did not seem to mind taking our money at all.

It was a Sunday when we arrived, and Sunday is the recognised day for races and sports in France. A French journal informed us that there was a day's racing to be held; so the next thing was to find out where the course was, and how to get there. With this object in view we went to a barber's shop — all the shops were wide open although it was Sunday — and in my best French I asked how one could get out to the course. The barber got me to repeat the sentence, and then said that they had a man in the shop who spoke German, but he was out at his lunch. I explained to the American what had happened, and he said, "I reckon that Australian French of yours doesn't go here. Let me at him!" Then, talking through his nose at the top of his voice, he said, "Whurrs the hoss race, sonny?" This only made the barber shrug up his shoulders and spread out his hands, and the American looked at him with supreme disgust. "He knows right enough," he said, "but he won't tell us! It's all on account of that Boer War of yours!" Then we went back to the hotel, and found out all about it from the "boots", who was — like the boots at hotels all the world over — an ardent sportsman. Perhaps it is because they are such ardent sportsmen that they are reduced to being "boots". After lunch we chartered a cab, drawn by a horse whose forelegs fairly tottered under him — I have seen some equine wrecks in my time, but nothing to approach the French cab horse — and drove out to the course, and all the inhabitants of Marseilles shut up their shops and came out also.

A day's racing in France is something to remember. In Australia racing is a business, and everyone who goes out goes with bent brows and an anxious mind, to try and unravel what is to him a serious problem. But with the Frenchman, a day's racing is a light-hearted holiday. He closes his shop at one o'clock, and goes out with his wife, in a trap drawn by a little fat pony with jingling bells and harness, and rattles away through the clear crisp air, with the dry aromatic smell of the autumn leaves all round, down the long avenue of sycamores out to the course. The tram cars, loaded with the happy, laughing crowds, go thundering along the streets. Motor cars rush past at a pace that would not be tolerated for an instant in any Australian or English community; on the seat of each motor car, alongside the driver, sits a large black French poodle, sagely contemplating the moving scene around him, and with the wind blowing through his whiskers as the car rushes along. Everyone is laughing, and everyone looks on the racing in a light-hearted way, quite foreign to our idea. They have left dull care behind them for the day, and they will back a horse because they like the look of his tail or the colours of his jockey, and then say it is treachery if they lose their money!

*Allez-vous-en!* Let her go, Gallagher! The trams roared, the motor cars whizzed, the little fat ponies were urged to their wildest pace, and amidst shouting, laughing, and bell-ringing we arrived at the course, a beautiful piece of natural turf, shut in by sycamores and hedgerows of various sorts. The track itself was very little prepared, but in all these countries the great rainfall and the natural grass make such turf as we poor drought-stricken people can only wonder at. The surroundings of racing in the old countries are less businesslike and more pleasant than in Australia. We drove in through the gates of the course, and left our trap standing in what we would call the "flat", while we went on into the grandstand and saddling paddock. Prices of admission were much the same as they are in Australia. The totalisators were at work in the saddling paddock, one being for a straight-out win and the other for a place. Some horses were being paraded round a turf ring, the turf ring being enclosed by a lot of drying sheds, and although the appointments were complete enough there was a lack of the businesslike formality about them which one notices with us. It was more like what we would call a picnic meeting. The horses were nearly all English bred, and were equal to any stock I have ever seen anywhere. They differed from our horses only in the matter of condition. It would make a Randwick trainer weep to see the condition in which these horses were sent out to race. Some of them were as fat as fools, prancing about the paddocks on their hind legs, led by their "trainers" — men who looked like sort of cross between a Sicilian bandit and an ice cream merchant.

Before getting out to the track we purchased a daily paper, which gave all the runners, and a collection of the "tips" of all the local newspapers, besides a set of "tips" of its own. After a struggle with the French idioms, I gathered that one horse in the first race had at one time shown good form but had since "*couru obscurément*". I thought this would probably be a good sort of horse to back, as I had had experience in Australia of horses that had run "obscurely" for a time, and then suddenly astonished their critics. The crowd was pretty thick, about as numerous as would be seen at a suburban meeting near Sydney. The ladies were in great numbers, gorgeously dressed, escorted by heavy French swells, who simply rioted in huge fur-lined overcoats, with great cuffs of fur running halfway up the arms. A few English visitors were present, looking at the proceedings with dull eyes, but the horses of one stable were trained by English trainers, and the bulk of the riders in the races were English or American jockeys. I asked one of the English trainers whether the horses ran to win, and his remarkable reply was, "Yes, they always try here. The owners are all French noblemen; they have lots of money and don't know nothing." On this comforting suggestion the American and I started to try to back winners, being guided solely by the condition of the horses, occasionally fortifying our opinions by reference to the tips in the daily paper.

The first race was for a prize of 2000 francs (about £80), and for a distance of 2200 metres (I should guess it at about a mile), and carrying 47 kilograms, which looked to me about eight stone seven. The horse that had "*couru obscurément*" was not a favourite on the totalisator, but then the French do not back horses on form, they back them because they belong to local owners, or to a Bonapartist, or to a pro-Boer, or for any other reason that strikes their erratic fancy. A horse belonging to an Englishman could not have found a backer in the crowd, though he were as good as Carbine. We decided to back the best-conditioned horse and away they went down to the post. There were four runners, three of the jockeys being American, riding in the real gilt-edged American style, which is even more forward than our Australian boys ever get. Our horse justified our judgment by going to the front with a solitary opponent hanging on to him. Half a furlong from home, our horse looked to be having the best of it and his jockey then put in an American "finish", that is to say, he lay flat down on the horse's neck, and struck out with his legs and arms exactly like a man swimming, making wild flaps in the air with his whip at the same time. He missed the horse altogether with the whip more often than he hit him. His opponent was ridden by a French jockey, in the ordinary way, and snatched a well-deserved victory by a neck. In the next, a selling race of 220 metres, we went for a very well-conditioned bay mare called Rentière, by Gonsalvo from Rentless, and therefore evidently English-bred. The mare won her race for us like the aristocrat she undoubtedly was, but the interest in the racing was as nothing compared to the amusement of watching the spectators. A dashing young Frenchman, with waxed moustache, tall hat and fur-lined coat, was sitting in the stand near us with a party of three superbly dressed ladies round him. As the horses started he fixed his glasses on the race and sprang to his feet, his face working with emotion. The ladies huddled together, and watched, with undisguised admiration, the tornado of passion that was racking the frame of their cavalier. He had backed a big chestnut horse, which was running well up with the leaders. The horses not being wound up for condition, it is usual for them to muddle away the first half of a race, first one leading and then another, and every time that this chestnut horse drew out to the lead the Frenchman's face lit up, his chest expanded, and he turned with the air of a conqueror to the timid females behind him, saying, "*Il gagne, il gagne!*" When the horse dropped back, an ashen grey hue spread over his countenance, and his hands trembled so that he could hardly hold the glasses.

Round the turn they came, the chestnut and Rentière fighting it out in the lead. Both boys got to work with their whips at the distance, and they raced home locked together. Every instant of that finish must have seemed a year to our French friend. He clutched the rail in front of him, and clenched his teeth, and fairly shook with the strain that was put on him, while the females never looked at the race but watched him in mute sympathy. As the horses flashed past the post, with his chestnut beaten by a neck, he dropped back on the seat with the air of a man whose hopes in life are crushed. He was too heartbroken to speak for a long time. It turned out afterwards that he had five francs (four and twopence) on the chestnut in the place totalisator, so that he saved his money, but it was the defeat of his judgment that annoyed him. We gathered afterwards, from what he said, that the defeat of the chestnut horse was solely due to treachery. After the race, the American wished to walk up into a part of the grandstand which was marked in large letters "*Défendu*", evidently being reserved for the committee or some such body. I told him he could not go up there, but he said he would like to see them stop him, and he started to march gaily up the stone steps. He had not got far before he was in altercation with a pink-trousered *gendarme*, who tried to shove him down the steps. The next minute he had the *gendarme* round the waist, there was a flash of pink trousers in the air, we heard the *gendarme*'s agonised cry of "*A moi!*" and the two rolled down the steps, locked in each other's arms. The authorities were going to arrest the American under the impression that he was English, but when they found that he was an American they apologised profusely to him, and a *douceur* to the unfortunate *gendarme* settled all the trouble.

While the racing was going on, the holiday-making crowd of workmen, with their wives and children, a merry-hearted, laughing mob, sat on the turf outside the course, but only separated from it by a broad deep ditch. Here they had just as good a view of the racing as anyone in the track, and they enjoyed the day thoroughly. That is the right way to go racing — to squirm and yell when your horse gets ahead, and prance about the paddock with an eagle-soaring step after a win of 1s 6d. The French do not know much about racing, but they get a lot of fun out of it. They take out a little basket full of cakes and lemonade, and the old father and mother sit in the sun on the grass while the children play about. They look at the racing just as we look at a race on the stage, merely as a spectator, and the entertainment doesn't cost them anything.

The day's sport was brought to a successful finish by a win in the last race by an English-bred, English-trained, and English-ridden horse, but, as he belonged to a local owner, a French *vicomte*, the crowd were quite satisfied, for they had all backed him, and they departed for home in the best of spirits.

The drive home was even more hilarious than the drive out. Everybody was laughing, shouting, and singing. We saw a horse run into by a motor car and killed on the spot, but the carcass was soon taken away, and everyone, including the owners of the horse, appeared to look upon the accident as an excellent jest. The crowd soon made their way back into their shops, and settled down for their next week's hard work, for the Frenchman lives in his shop, and his shop is open all the time that he is at home.

The best prizes for the racing were given by a society for the encouragement of horse breeding. Steeplechasing, that test of stamina and endurance, is at a very much higher level in France than in England, and there is not much doubt that the French do try to make racing a means to improving the breed of horses. Someday in Australia we may come to look at it in the same way.

## A Series of Racing Specials.
(Drawn for "The Comic Australian" by STUART ALLAN.)
No 2

"Jumpin' Geerusalem! But this is the joy ride of my life."

LEFT AT THE POST.

# From *Motoring* to *Melbourne*

## ENGLISH MOTORING

And right here it is worthwhile to say a little about motoring in England. The roads in England require to be seen to be believed. Even narrow little country lanes, overhung by great oaks, and littered ankle-deep in leaves, even these have a surface as smooth as glass, whereon the motorist can let her out to his heart's content, drawing the leaves and dust to a whirlwind after him. Down about Brighton, which is the happy hunting ground of the London motorist, in dry weather each car flies along, raising a cloud of dust that moves like the pillar of fire that guided the Israelites, but a trifle faster. And it is just the excellence of the roads that has made the motorist so unpopular in England. When a man has got a machine under him that can travel at thirty miles an hour and a good road to run her on, it isn't in human nature to throttle her down to six miles an hour. So they let her out and the Bumbles and Parish Council prosecute and fine them relentlessly, planting policemen in the hedges to take the time of the flying motors from one milestone to another, and the motor clubs pay men to track out these policemen and to stand outside their hiding places and wave a red flag, so that the motorist can see where the danger lies and can slow up in time.

## SHAVING THE "COPPERS"

In rural England they do not love the motorist. The local squire, who has never been hurried in his life, is condescending to cross the village street at his usual leisurely strut, when "booh! booh! whizz!" a motor is all but over him, and he has to skip in a very undignified way for the sidewalk if he wishes to save his precious life. Giles Jollyfowl, the farmer, taking a load of manure home, sleeps peaceably on top of his load as usual, and lets the old horses go their own way. Next thing there is an appalling whizz and a racing Panhard or Gladiator tears past like a long streak through the atmosphere, the old horses wheel round, and rush off the road, and Giles Jollyfowl finds himself in the ditch with his load of manure on top of him. That is why the English papers are full of complaints against motorists. They don't like being hurried in

England. But the motorist is a good deal to blame, for a sort of professional pride exists among gentlemen motorists and their chauffeurs, and it is considered *de rigueur* to drive full speed just where the traffic is thickest, to cut corners by the merest hairsbreadth, to graze vehicles as closely as possible in passing — just to teach them to give a bit more room another time — and, above all, always to pass a traffic constable so close as almost to shave the buttons off his uniform. They are great people for "the correct thing" in England, and "the correct thing" in motoring is to make all created things step lively when you are on the road.

## THE MOTOR RIG-OUT

By common consent, breeches and gaiters similar to those used for riding, seem to be adopted as the correct motor costume. Add to these a high-peaked cap, a white macintosh, a pair of awful goggles, and possibly a mask with a false leather nose, and you have some idea of the visitors who are stirring up the City of Goulburn at the time of writing.

There is a famous expression used by Mark Twain in the *Innocents Abroad* — "We made Rome howl." That is just what the motorists are doing here. They are making Goulburn howl. From 11.52, when H. L. Stevens' Darracq car rushed into Goulburn ahead of the ruck, up till 4 p.m., the main street has been blocked by a singing, jabbering, mass of small boys, agriculturists, and local oracles, all explaining to each other all about motor cars. As each fresh car comes in there is a wild rush, and the small boys push each other nearly under the wheels, and just as the throng is thickest a Yankee driver, with a face like granite, sends two thousand pounds' weight of priceless mechanism in amongst them, and the mob scatters and drifts up and down the street, fingering the cars that are waiting by the roadside filling up and making adjustments before being handed over. Each fresh chauffeur is a thing of less beauty than the last, and Goulburn has not got reconciled to their peaked caps, their goggles, and their iron features. One hears of bicycle face. Motor face is the same, but a good deal harder. Concentrated watchfulness is the essence of the motor face — the watchfulness of the man who may hit a drain, or take a side-slip and spin off the road at any moment and land in the ditch with a lot of nearly red-hot machinery on top of him. They say the crack drivers in the old country have to be in full training to do one of their long speed runs, and when one sees the wreck that can be made by the hundredth of a second's carelessness, one can easily believe it.

## The Reliability Trial
### Part III

Friday February 24

It is a "reliability" trial sure enough. The second day's run was enough to fix that in the minds of the competitors. Eighteen miles an hour over bush roads tries the best car, and there is a lot of luck needed to get through. The extra speed necessitates driving for all she is worth on the level, and if the level happens to be bisected by a drain, you haven't time to step out; must just bump over it. The result is that constant bumping and straining weakens the axles, and the wheels begin to lean in towards each other. Quite three-fourths of the competing cars are "developing bowed tendons", as the racing men would say. The axles are all bending a little. And coming round sharp curves through loose metal causes a side strain that sooner or later tells on the wheels. Two cars today — Messrs Rand's and Langford's — pulled their wheels right off. Of course, an occasional "interesting adventure with cattle" is met with, but nothing of a serious character.

In fact, disasters began early, as the lady competitor — Mrs Thompson — got into difficulties soon after leaving Goulburn. The French demon driver, who has so far formed the chief topic of conversation on the trip, came to some sort of grief at Gunning. We passed him, but, as Mr Jorrocks says, the pace was too good to inquire. From Goulburn to Yass you get the best bit of road we have seen so far; and being delayed soon after the start, we had to make the most of that bit of road.

# Three Elephant Power

## A Motor Story

"THEM THINGS", said Alfred the chauffeur, tapping the speed indicator with his finger, "them things are all right for the police. But, Lord, you can fix 'em up if you want to. Did you ever hear about Henery, that used to drive for old John Bull — Henery and the ellyphunt?"

Alfred was chauffeur to a friend of mine, a friend who owned a very powerful car, and Alfred was part of the car. He was an Australian youth. It is strange that in Australia the motor has already produced the motor type. Weirdly intelligent, of poor physique, Alfred might have been any age from fifteen to eighty. His education had been somewhat hurried, but there was no doubt as to his mechanical ability. He took to a car like a young duck to water. He talked motor, and thought motor, and would have accepted with — well, I won't say enthusiasm, for Alfred's motto was *Nil admirari* — but without hesitation, an offer to drive in the greatest race in the world. He could drive really well, too, and as for belief in himself, after six months' apprenticeship in a garage, he was prepared to vivisect a six-cylinder engine with the confidence of a diplomaed Bachelor of Engineering.

Barring a tendency to flash driving and a delight in "persecuting" slow cars by driving just in front of them and letting them come up and enjoy his dust, and then shooting away again, he was a very respectable member of society. When his "boss" was in the car he cloaked the natural ferocity of his instincts; but this day, with only myself as passenger on board, and a clear run of 120 miles up to the station before him, he let her loose, confident that if any trouble occurred I would be held morally responsible.

As we fled past a somnolent bush public house, Alfred, whistling softly, leant forward and turned on a little more oil.

"You never heard about Henery and the ellyphunt?" he said. "It was dead funny. Henery was a bushwacker, but clean mad on motorin'. He was wood and water joey at some squatter's place you know, and he seen a motor car go past one day, the first that ever they had in the districk. 'That's my game,' says Henery; 'no more wood and water joey for me.' So he comes to town and gets a job off Miles that had that garage at the back of Allison's. And an old cove that they call John Bull — I don't know his right name, he was a fat old cove — he used to come there to hire cars, and Henery used to drive him. And this old John Bull he had lots of stuff, so at last he reckons he's going to get a car for himself, and he promises Henery a job to drive it. A queer cove this Henery was — half mad, I think — but the best hand with a car ever I see."

While he had been talking we topped a hill and opened up a new stretch of blue-grey granite like road. Down at the foot of the hill before us was a teamster's waggon in camp: the horses in their harness munching at their nose bags, while the teamster and a mate were boiling a billy a little off to the side of the road. There was a turn in the road just below the waggon which looked a bit sharp, so of course Alfred bore down on it like a whirlwind. The big stupid team horses huddled together and pushed each other awkwardly as we passed. A dog that had been sleeping in the shade of the waggon sprang out from beneath it right in front of the car, and was exterminated without ever knowing what struck him. There was just room to clear the tail of the waggon to negotiate the turn, and as Alfred, with the calm decision of a Napoleon, swung round the bend, he found that the old teamster's hack, fast asleep, was tied to the tail of the waggon, and nothing but a most lightning-like twist of the steering wheel prevented our scooping the old animal up, and taking him on board as a passenger. As it was, we got a lot of his tail as a trophy caught on the brass of the lamp. The old steed, thus rudely awakened, lashed out good and hard, but by the time he kicked we were gone and he missed the car by a quarter of a mile. During this strenuous episode, Alfred never relaxed his professional stolidity, and when we were clear he went on with his story in the tone of a man who found life wanting in animation.

"Well, at first, the old man would only buy one of these little eight-horse rubby dubbys that used to go strugglin' up the 'ills with the death rattle in its throat, and all the people in buggies passin' it. And o' course that didn't suit Henery. He used to get that spiked when a car passed him he'd nearly go mad. And one day he nearly got the sack for dodging his car about up a steep 'ill in front of one o' them big twenty-four Darracqs, full of 'owlin' toffs, and wouldn't let 'em get a chance to go past till they got to the top of the 'ill. But at last he persuaded old John Bull to let him go to England and buy a car for him. He was to do a year in the shops, and pick up all the wrinkles and get a car for the old man. Bit better than wood and water joeying, wasn't it?"

Our progress here was barred by our rounding a corner right onto a flock of sheep, that at once packed together into a solid mass in front of us, blocking the whole road from fence to fence. "Silly cows o' things, ain't they?" said Alfred, putting on his emergency brake, and skidding up till the car softly came to rest against the cushion-like mass — a much quicker stop than any horse-drawn vehicle could have made in the time. A few sheep were crushed somewhat, but it is well known that a sheep is practically indestructible by violence. Whatever Alfred's faults were, he could certainly drive.

"Well," he went on, lighting a cigarette, unheeding the growls of the drovers, who were trying to get the sheep to pass the car, "well, as I was sayin', Henery went to England, and he got a car. Do you know wot he got?"

"No, I don't."

" 'E got a ninety," said Alfred, giving time for the words to soak in.

"A ninety! What do you mean?"

" 'E got a ninety — a ninety-horse power racin' engine that was made for some American millionaire, and wasn't as fast as wot some other millionaire had, so he sold it for the price of the iron, and Henery got it, and had a body built for it, and he come out here, and tells us all it's a twenty mongrel — you know, one of them cars that's made part in one place and part in another, the body here and the engine there, and the radiator another place. There's lots of cheap cars made like that. So Henery he says that this is a twenty mongrel — only a four-cylinder engine — and nobody drops to what she is till Henery goes out one Sunday and waits for the big Napier that Scotty used to drive — it belonged to the same bloke that owned that big racehorse what won all the races. So Henery and Scotty they have a fair go round the park while both their bosses is at church, and Henery beat him out o' sight — fair lost him — and so Henery was reckoned the boss of the road. No one would take him on after that."

A nasty creek crossing here required all Alfred's attention. A little girl, carrying a billy can of water, stood by the stepping stones, and smiled shyly as we passed, and Alfred waved her a salute quite as though he were an ordinary human being. I felt comforted. He had his moments of relaxation, evidently, and his affections the same as other people.

"And what happened to Henery and ninety-horse machine?" I said. "Where does the elephant come in? For a chauffeur, you're a long time coming to the elephant."

Alfred smiled pityingly.

"Ain't I tellin' yer?" he said. "You wouldn't understand if I didn't tell yer how he got the car and all that. So here's Henery," he went on, "with old John Bull goin' about in the fastest car in Australia, and old John, he's a quiet old geezer, that wouldn't drive faster than the regulations for anything, and he's that short-sighted he can't see to the side of the road. So what does Henery do, but he fixes the speed indicator — puts a new face on it, so that when the car is doing thirty, the indicator only shows fifteen, and twenty for forty and so on. So out they'd go and if Henery knew there was a big car in front of him, he'd let out to forty-five, and the pace would very near blow the whiskers off old John, and every now and again he'd look at the indicator, and it'd be showin' twenty-two and a half, and he'd say, 'Better be careful, Henery, you're slightly exceedin' the speed limit; twenty miles an hour, you know, Henery, should be fast enough for anybody, and you're doing over twenty-two.' And one day, Henery told me he was tryin' to catch up a big car that just came out from France, and it had a half-hour start of him, and he was just fairly flyin', an' there was a lot of cars on the road, and he flies past 'em so fast the old man says, 'It's very strange, Henery,' he says, 'that all the cars that are out to-day are comin' this way,' he says. You see he was passin' 'em so fast he thought they were all comin' towards him. And Henery sees a mate of his coming, so he lets out a notch or two, and the two cars flew by each other like chain lightnin'. They were each doin' about forty, and the old man, he says, 'There's a driver must be travellin' a hundred miles an hour,' he says, 'I never see a car go by so fast in my life,' he says. 'If I could find out who he is, I'd report him,' he says. 'Did you know the car, Henery?' But of course Henery, he doesn't know, so on they goes. And when they caught the French car — the owner of it thinks he has the fastest car in Australia — and Henery and the old man are seen coming, he tells his driver to let her out a little, but Henery gives the ninety-horse the full of the lever, and whips up alongside in one jump. And then he keeps there just half a length ahead of him, tormentin' him, like. And the owner of the French car he yowls out to old John Bull, 'You're goin' a nice pace for an old 'un,' he says. Old John has a blink down at the indicator. 'We're doing twenty-five,' he yells out. 'Twenty-five grandmothers,' says the bloke; but Henery put on his accelerator and left him. It wouldn't do to let the old man get wise to it, you know."

We topped a big hill, and Alfred cut off the engine and let the car swoop as swiftly and as noiselessly as an eagle down to the flat country below.

"You're a long while coming to the elephant, Alfred," I said.

"Well, now, I'll tell you about the ellyphunt," said Alfred, letting his clutch in again, and taking up the story to the accompaniment of the rhythmic throb of the engine. "One day Henery and the old man were going a long trip over the mountain, and down the Kangaroo Valley road that's all cut out of the side of the 'ill. And after they's gone a mile or two, Henery sees a track in the road — the track of the biggest car he ever saw or heard of. An' the more he looks at it, the more he reckons he must ketch that car and see what's she made of. So he slows down passin' two yokels on the road, and he says, 'Did you see a big car along 'ere?' 'Yes, we did,' they says. 'How big is she?' says Henery.

'Biggest car ever we see,' says the yokels, and they laughed that silly way these yokels always does.

"'How many horsepower do you think she was?' says Henery.

"'Horse power,' they says; 'elephant power you mean! she was three elephant power!' they says; and they goes, 'Haw, haw' and Henery drops his clutch in, and off he goes after that car.'"

Alfred lit another cigarette as a preliminary to the climax.

"So they run for miles, and all the time there's the track ahead of 'em, and Henery keeps lettin' her out, thinkin' that he'll never ketch that car. They went through a town so fast, the old man he says, 'What house was that we just passed?' he says. So at last they come to the top of the big 'ill, and there's the tracks of the big car goin' straight down ahead of 'em. D'you know that road? It's all cut out of the side of the mountain, and there's places where if she was to side-slip you'd go down 'undreds of thousands of feet. And there's sharp turns, too, but the surface is good, so Henery he lets her out, and down they go, whizzin' round the turns and skatin' out near the edge, and the old cove sittin' there enjoyin' it, never knowin' the danger. And comin' to one turn Henery gives a toot on the 'orn, and then he heard somethin' go 'Toot, toot' right away down the mountain. 'Bout a mile ahead it seemed to be, and Henery reckoned he'd go another four miles before he'd ketch it, so he chances them turns more than ever. And she was pretty hot, too; but he kept her at it, and he hadn't gone a full mile till he come round a turn about forty miles an hour, and before he could stop he run right into it, and wot do you think it was?"

I hadn't the faintest idea.

"A circus. One of them travellin' circuses, goin' down the coast, and one of the ellyphunts had sore feet, so they put him in a big waggon and another ellyphunt pulled in front and one pushed behind. Three ellyphunt power it was, right enough. That was the waggon that made the big track. Well, it was all done so sudden. Before Henery could stop, he runs the radiator — very near boiling she was — up against the ellyphunt's tail, and prints the pattern of the latest honeycomb radiator on the ellyphunt as clear as if you done it with a stencil plate. And the ellyphunt, he lets a roar out of him like one of them bulls bellerin', and he puts out his nose and ketches Henery round the neck, and yanks him out of the car, and chucks him right clean over the cliff, 'bout a thousand feet. But he never done nothin' to the old bloke."

"Good gracious!"

"Well, it finished Henery, killed him stone dead, of course, and the old man he was terrible cut up over losin' such a steady, trustworthy man. Never get another like him, he says."

We were nearly at our journey's end, and we turned through a gate into the home paddocks. Some young stock, both horses and cattle,

# THE Comic Australian

Registered at the G.P.O. for transmission by Post as a Newspaper.

## A JOURNAL OF FACT, FUN, AND FICTION.

Vol. 2, No. 33.　　　　　MAY 14, 1912.　　　　　Price, One Penny.

(On Hospital Saturday one of the elephants from Wirths' Circus visited the hotels in the neighbourhood with a collection box.—News Item.)

"Great snakes! I've got 'em again worse than ever."

( On Hospital Saturday one of the elephants from Wirths' Circus
visited the hotels in the neighbourhood with a collection box. – News It
" Great snakes! I've got 'em again worse then ever. "

came frisking and cantering after the car, and the rough bush track took all Alfred's attenton. We crossed a creek, the water swishing from the wheels, and began the long pull up to the homestead. Over the clamour of the little-used second speed, Alfred concluded his narrative.

"The old bloke advertised," he said, "for another driver, a steady reliable man to drive a twenty-horse power, four-cylinder touring car. An' every driver in Sydney put in for it. Nothing like a fast car to fetch 'em, you know. And Scotty got it. Him that used to drive the Napier I was tellin' you about."

"And what did the old man say when he found he'd been running a racing car?"

"He don't know now. Scotty never told 'im. Why should he? He's drivin' about the country now, the boss of the roads, but he won't chance her near a circus. Thinks he might bump the same ellyphunt. And they reckon that ellyphunt, when he's in the circus, every time he smells a car passin' in the road, he goes near mad with fright. If he ever sees that car again, do you think he'd know it?"

Not being used to the capacities of elephants, I could not offer an opinion.

THE QUICK OR THE DEAD.

# The Downfall
# of Mulligan's

THE SPORTING men of Mulligan's were an exceedingly knowing lot: in fact, they had obtained the name amongst their neighbours of being a little bit too knowing. They had "taken down" the sporting men of the adjoining town in a variety of ways. They were always winning maiden plates with horses which were shrewdly suspected to be old and well-tried performers in disguise. When the sports of Paddy's Flat unearthed a phenomenal runner in the shape of a blackfellow called Frying-Pan Joe, the Mulligan contingent immediately took the trouble to discover a blackfellow of their own, and they made a match and won all the Paddy's Flat money with ridiculous ease; then their blackfellow turned out to be a well-known Sydney performer. They had a man who could fight, a man who could be backed to jump five feet ten, a man who could kill eight pigeons out of nine at thirty yards, a man who could make a break of fifty or so at billiards if he tried; they could all drink, and they all had that indefinite look of infinite wisdom and conscious superiority which belongs only to those who know something about horseflesh. They knew a great many things which they never learnt at a Sunday school; at cards and such things they were perfect adepts; they would go to immense trouble to work off a small swindle in a sporting line, and the general consensus of opinion was that they were a very "fly" crowd at Mulligan's, and if you went there you wanted to "keep your eyes skinned" or they'd "have" you over a threepenny bit.

There were races at Sydney one Christmas, and a chosen and select band of the Mulligan sportsmen were going down to them. They were in high feather, having just won a lot of money from a young Englishman at pigeon shooting, by the simple yet ingenious method of slipping blank cartridges into his gun when he wasn't looking, and then backing the bird; also they knew several dead certainties for the races. They intended to make a fortune out of the Sydney people before they came back, and their admirers who came to see them off only asked them as a favour to leave money enough among the Sydney crowd to make it worth while for another detachment to go down later on. Just as the train was departing a priest came running on to the platform, and was bundled by the porters into the carriage where our Mulligan friends were, the door was slammed to, and away they went. His Reverence was hot and perspiring, and for a few minutes he mopped himself with a handkerchief, while the silence was unbroken except by the rattle of the train.

After a while one of the Mulligan fraternity got out a pack of cards and proposed a game to while away the time. There was a young squatter in the carriage who looked as if he might be induced to lose a few pounds, and the sportsmen thought they would be neglecting their opportunities if they did not try and "get a bit to go on with" from him. He agreed to play, and just as a matter of courtesy, they asked the priest whether he would take a hand.

"What game d'ye play?" he asked, in a melodious brogue. They explained that any game was equally acceptable to them, but they thought it right to add that they generally played for money. "Shure an' it don't matter for wanst in a way," sez he — "Oi'll take a hand bedad — I'm only going about fifty miles, so I can't lose a fortune." Then they lifted a light portmanteau onto their knees to make a table, and five of them — three of the Mulligan's crowd and the two strangers — started to have a little game of poker. Things looked rosy for the Mulligan's boys and they chuckled as they thought how soon they were making a beginning, and what a magnificent yarn they would have to tell about how they rooked the priest on the way down.

Nothing very sensational resulted from the first few deals, and the priest began to ask questions of the others. "Be ye going to the races?" he enquired. They said that they were. "Ah! and I suppose ye'll be betting with these bookmakers — bettin' on the horses, will yez! They do be terrible knowing men, these bookmakers, they tell me. I wouldn't bet much if I was ye," he said, with an affable smile. "If ye go bettin' ye will be took in with these bookmakers." The boys from Mulligan's listened with a bored air and reckoned that by the time they parted the priest would have learnt that they were well able to look after themselves. They went steadily on with the game, and the priest and the young squatter won slightly; this was part of the plan to lead them on to the plunge. They neared the station where the priest was to get out. He had won something rather more than they liked, and the signal was passed round to "put the cross on" — i.e., to manipulate the hands so as to get back his winnings and let him go. Poker is a game at which a man need not risk much unless he feels inclined, and on this deal the priest chose not to risk anything and stood out; consequently when they drew up at the station he still had a few pounds of their money. He half rose and then he said: "Bedad, and I don't like going away with yer money. Oi'll go on to the next station so as ye can have revenge." Then he sat down again, and the play went on in earnest.

The man of religion seemed to have the Devil's own luck. When he was dealt a good hand he invariably backed it well, and if he had a bad one he would not risk anything. The sports grew painfully anxious as they saw him getting further and further ahead of them, prattling away and joking all the time like a big schoolboy. The squatter was the biggest loser so far as they had got, but the priest was the only winner. All the others were out of pocket. His Reverence played with great dash, and seemed to know a lot about the game; and when they arrived at the second station he was in pocket a good round sum. He rose to leave them, with many expressions of regret at having robbed them of their money, and laughingly promising full revenge next time. Just as he was opening the door of the carriage, one of the Mulligan's fraternity said in a stage whisper, "I thought that was how it would be. He's a sinkpocket, and won't give us our revenge now. If he can come this far, let him come on to Sydney and play for double the stakes." The priest heard the remark and turned quickly round. "Bedad, an' if *that's* yer talk, Oi'll go on wid yez and play ye fer double stakes from here to the other side of glory. Play on, now! Do yez think men are mice because they eat cheese? It isn't one of the Ryans would be fearing to give any man his revenge!" He snorted defiance at them, grabbed his cards and waded in. The others felt that a crisis was at hand and settled down to play in a dead silence. The priest kept on winning steadily. The gamblers saw that something decisive must be done, and the leader of the party, the "old man" — "The Daddy" as they put it — decided to make a big plunge and get all the money back on one hand. By a dexterous manipulation of the cards, which luckily was undetected, he dealt himself four kings, almost the best hand at poker. Then he began with assumed hesitation to bet on his hand; he kept raising the stake little by little until the priest exclaimed, "Sure yez are trying to bluff, so ye are!" and immediately started raising it on his part. The others had dropped out of the game and watched with painful interest the stake grow and grow. The Mulligan fraternity felt a cheerful certainty that the "old man" had made everything secure, and they looked upon themselves as mercifully delivered from a very unpleasant situation. The priest went on doggedly raising the stake in response to his antagonist's challenges until it had attained huge dimensions. Then he said, "Sure, that's high enough," and he put into the pool sufficient to entitle him to see his opponent's hand. The "old man" with great gravity laid down his four kings; the Mulligan boys let a big sigh of relief escape them; they were saved — he surely couldn't beat four kings. Then the priest laid down four aces and scooped the pool.

The sportsmen of Mulligan's never quite knew how they got out to Randwick to the races. They borrowed a bit of money in Sydney and found themselves in the saddling paddock in a half-dazed condition trying to realise what had happened to them. During the afternoon they were up at the end of the lawn near the Leger stand, and from that enclosure they could hear the babel of tongues, the small bookmakers, pea-and-thimble men, confidence men, plying their trades. In the tumult of voices they heard one which seemed familiar. After a while suspicion became certainty, and they knew that it was the voice of Father Ryan, who had cleaned them out. They walked to the fence and looked over. They could hear his voice distinctly, and this is what he was saying, "Pop it down, gents! Pop it down! If you don't put down a brick you can't pick up a castle! I'll bet no one here can find the knave of hearts out of these three cards. I'll bet half-a-sovereign no one here can find the knave!" Then the crowd parted a little, and through the opening they could see him distinctly — a three-card man — doing a great business and showing wonderful dexterity with the pasteboard.

This was the downfall of Mulligan's. There is still enough money in Sydney to make it worthwhile for another detachment of knowing sportsmen to come down from that city; but the next lot will hesitate about playing cards with strangers in the train.

# The Cast-Iron
# Canvasser

T HE FIRM of Sloper and Dodge, book publishers and printers, was in great distress. These two enterprising individuals had worked up an enormous business in time payment books, which they sold all over Australia by means of canvassers. They had put a lot of money into the business — all they had, in fact. And now, just as everything was in thorough working order, the public had revolted against them. Their canvassers were ill-treated and molested by the country folk in all sorts of strange bush ways. One man was made drunk, and then a two-horse harrow was run over him; another was decoyed out into the desolate ranges on pretence of being shown a gold mine, and then his guide galloped away and left him to freeze all night in the bush. In mining localities, on the appearance of a canvasser, the inhabitants were called together by beating a camp oven lid with a pick, and the canvasser was given ten minutes to leave the town alive. If he disregarded the hint he would as likely as not fall accidentally down a disused shaft. The people of one district applied to their member of Parliament to have canvassers brought under the Noxious Animals Act and demanded that a reward should be offered for their scalps. Reports were constantly published in the country press about strange, gigantic birds that appeared at remote free selections, and frightened the inhabitants to death — these were Sloper and Dodge's sober and reliable agents, wearing the neat, close-fitting suits of tar and feathers with which their enthusiastic yokel admirers had presented them. In fact, it was too hot altogether for the canvassers, and they came in from north and west and south, crippled and disheartened, and handed in their resignations. To make matters worse, Sloper and Dodge had just got out a map of Australasia on a great scale, and if they couldn't sell it, ruin stared them in the face; and how could they sell it without canvassers!

The two members of the firm sat in their private office. Sloper was a long, sanctimonious individual, very religious and very bald — "beastly, awfully bald". Dodge was a little, fat American, with bristly black hair and beard, and quick, beady eyes. He was eternally smoking a reeking black pipe, and swallowing the smoke, and then puffing it out through his nose in great whiffs, like a locomotive on a steep grade. Anybody walking into one of those whiffs incautiously was likely to get paralysed, the tobacco was so strong.

As the firm waited, Dodge puffed nervously at his pipe and filled the office with noxious fumes. The two partners were in a very anxious and expectant condition.

Just as things were at their very blackest, an event had happened which promised to relieve all their difficulties. An inventor, a genius, had come forward, who offered to supply the firm with a patent cast-iron canvasser, a figure which he said when wound up would walk about, talk by means of a phonograph, collect orders, and stand any amount of ill usage and wear and tear. If this could indeed be done, then they were saved. They had made an appointment with the genius to inspect his figure, but he was half an hour late, and the partners were steeped in gloom.

Just as they despaired of his appearing at all, a cab rattled up to the door, and Sloper and Dodge rushed unanimously to the window. A young man, very badly dressed, stepped out of the cab, holding over his shoulder what looked like the upper half of a man's body. In his disengaged hand he held a pair of human legs with boots and trousers on. Thus equipped he turned to the cabman to ask his fare, but the man with a yell of terror whipped up his horse, and disappeared at a hand gallop, and a woman who happened to be going by went howling down the street, saying that "Jack the Ripper" had come to town. The man bolted in at the door, and toiled up the dark stairs, tramping heavily under his hideous load, the legs and feet which he dragged after him making an unearthly clatter. He came in and put his burden down on the sofa.

"There you are, gents," he said. "There's your canvasser."

Sloper and Dodge recoiled in horror. The upper part of the man had a waxy face, dull, fishy eyes, and dark hair; he lounged on the sofa like a corpse at ease, while his legs and feet stood by, leaning stiffly against the wall. The partners looked at him for a while in silence, and felt like two men haunted by a cast-iron ghost.

"Fix him together, for God's sake," said Dodge. "Don't leave him like that — he looks awful."

The genius grinned, and soon fixed the legs on.

"Now he looks better," said Dodge, poking about the figure "Looks as much like life as most — ah, would you, you brute!" he exclaimed, springing back in alarm, for the figure had made a violent La Blanche swing at him.

"That's all right," said the genius, "that's a notion of my own. It's no good having his face knocked about, you know — lot of trouble to make that face. His head and body are all full of concealed springs, and if anybody hits him in the countenance, or in the pit of the stomach — favourite place to hit canvassers, the pit of the stomach — it sets a strong spring in motion, and he fetches his right hand round with a swipe that'll knock them into the middle of next week. It's an awful hit. Griffo couldn't dodge it, and Slavin couldn't stand against it. No fear of any man hitting *him* twice. And he's dog-proof too. His legs are padded with tar and oakum, and if a dog bites a bit out of him, it will take that dog the rest of his life to pick his teeth clean. Never bite anybody again, that dog won't. And he'll talk, talk, talk, like a pious conference gone mad; his phonograph can be charged for 100,000 times, and all you've got to do is to speak into it what you want him to say, and he'll say it. He'll go on saying it till he talks his man silly, or gets an order. He has an order form in his hand, and as soon as anyone signs it and gives it back to him, that sets another spring in motion, and he puts the order in his pocket, turns round, and walks away. Grand idea isn't he? Lor' bless you, I fairly love him."

Evidently he did, for as he spoke the genius grinned affectionately at his monster.

"What about stairs?" said Dodge.

"No stairs in the bush," said the inventor blowing a speck of dust off his apparition, "all ground floor houses. Anyhow, if there were stairs we could carry him up and let him fall down afterwards, or get flung down like any other canvasser."

"Ha! Let's see him walk," said Dodge.

The figure walked all right, stiff and erect.

"Now let's hear him yabber," was the next order.

Immediately the genius touched a spring, and a queer, tin-whistly voice issued from the creature's lips, and he began to sing, "Little Annie Rooney."

"Good!" said Dodge, "he'll do. We'll give you your price. Leave him here tonight, and come in tomorrow, and we'll start you off to some place in the back country with him. Have a cigar."

And Mr Dodge, much elated, sucked at his pipe, and blew out through his nose a cloud of nearly solid smoke, which hung and floated about the door, and into which the genius walked as he sidled off. It fairly staggered him, and they could hear him sneezing and choking all the way downstairs. Then they locked up the office, and made for home, leaving the figure in readiness for his travels on the ensuing day.

Ninemile was a quiet little place, sleepy beyond description. When the mosquitoes in that town settled on anyone, they usually went to sleep, and forgot to bite him. The climate was so hot that the very grasshoppers used to crawl into the hotel parlours out of the sun. There they would climb up the window curtains and go to sleep, and if

**AS PER SAMPLE.**

Canvasser: "If you have a small photo of yourself we should be pleased to make you an enlargement from it, exactly the same as this."

anybody disturbed them they would fly into his eye with a great whizz, and drive the eye clean out at the back of his head. There was no likelihood of a public riot at Ninemile. The only thing that could rouse the inhabitants out of their lethargy was the prospect of a drink at somebody else's expense. And for those reasons it was decided to start the canvasser in this forgotten region; and then move him on to more populous and active localities if he proved a success. They sent up the genius, and a companion who knew the district well. The genius was to manage the automaton, and the other was to lay out the campaign, choose the victims, and collect the money, if they got any, geniuses being notoriously unreliable and loose in their cash. They got through a good deal of whisky on the way up, and when they arrived at Ninemile, they were in a cheerful mood, and disposed to take risks.

"Who'll we begin on?" said the genius.

"Oh, d —— it," said the other, "let's start on Macpherson."

Macpherson was the big bug of the place. He was a gigantic Scotchman, six feet four in his socks, freckled all over with freckles as big as half-crowns. His eyebrows would have been made decent-sized moustaches even for a cavalryman, and his moustaches looked like horns. He was a fighter, from the ground up, and, moreover, he had a desperate "down" on canvassers generally and on Sloper and Dodge's canvassers in particular. This eminent firm had once published a book called *Remarkable Colonials*, and Macpherson had written out his own biography for it. He was intensely proud of his pedigree, and his grand relations, and in his narrative made out that he was descended from the original Pherson or Fhairshon who swam round Noah's Ark with his title deeds in his teeth. He showed how his people had fought under Alexander the Great and Timour, and had come over to England some centuries before the Conqueror. He also proved that he was related in a general way to one emperor, fifteen kings, twenty-five dukes, and earls and lords and viscounts innumerable. He dilated on the splendour of the family estates in Scotland, and the vast wealth of his relatives and progenitors. And then, after all, Sloper and Dodge managed to mix him up with some other fellow, some lowbred Irish ruffian who drove a corporation cart! Macpherson's biography gave it forth to the astonished town that he was born in Dublin of poor but honest parents, that his father when a youth had lived by selling matches, until one day he chanced to pick up a cigar end, and, emboldened by the possession of so much capital, had got married, and the product was Macpherson.

It was a terrible outrage. Macpherson at once because president for the whole of the western districts of the *Remarkable Colonials* Defence League, the same being a fierce and homicidal association got up to resist, legally and otherwise, paying for the books. Also, he had sworn by all he held sacred that every canvasser who came to harry him in future should die, and he had put up a notice on his office door, "Canvassers come in here at their own risk". He had a dog which he called a dog of the "hold 'em" breed, and this dog could tell a canvasser by his walk, and would go for him on sight. The reader will understand, therefore, that when the genius and his mate proposed to start on Macpherson, they were laying out a capacious contract for the cast-iron canvasser, and were taking a step which could only have been inspired by a morbid craving for excitement, aided by the influence of back block whisky.

The genius wound the figure up in the back parlour of the pub. There were a frightful lot of screws to tighten before the thing would work, but at last he said it was ready, and they shambled off down the street, the figure marching stiffly between them. It had a book stuck under its arm and an order form in its hand. When they arrived opposite Macpherson's office (he was a land agent and had a ground-floor room) the genius started the phonograph working, pointed the figure straight at Macpherson's door and set it going, and then the two conspirators waited like Guy Fawkes in his cellar.

The figure marched across the road and in at the open door, talking to itself loudly in a hoarse, unnatural voice.

Macpherson was writing at his table and looked up.

The figure walked bang through a small collection of flower-pots, sent a chair flying, tramped heavily in the spittoon, and then brought up against the table with a loud crash and stood still. It was talking all the time.

"I have here," it said, "a most valuable work, a map and geography of Australia, which I desire to submit to your notice. The large and increasing demand of bush residents for time payment works has induced the publishers of this —"

"My God!" said Macpherson, "it's a canvasser. Here, Tom Sayers, Tom Sayers!" and he whistled and called for the dog. "Now," he said, "will you go out of this office quietly, or will you be thrown out? It's for yourself to decide, but you've only got while a duck wags his tail to decide in. Which'll it be?"

— "works of modern ages," said the canvasser. "Every person subscribing to this invaluable work will receive, in addition, a flat-iron, a railway pass for a year, and a pocket compass. If you will please sign this order —"

Just here Tom Sayers, the bulldog, came tearing through the office, and, without waiting for orders, hitched straight onto the calf of the canvasser's leg. To Macpherson's intense amazement the piece came clear away, and Tom Sayers rolled about the floor with his mouth full of some sticky substance which seemed to surprise him badly.

The long Scotchman paused awhile before this mystery, but at last he fancied he had got the solution. "Got a cork leg, have you?" said he. — "Well, let's see if your ribs are cork, too," and he struck the canvasser a terrific blow on the fifth button of the waistcoat.

Quicker than the lightning's flash came that terrific right-handed cross-counter. It was so quick that Macpherson never even knew what happened to him. He remembered striking his blow, and afterwards all was a blank. As a matter of fact, the canvasser's right hand, which had been adjusted by the genius for a high blow, landed just on the butt of Macpherson's ear and dropped him like a fowl. The gasping and terrified bulldog fled from the scene, and the canvasser stood over his fallen foe and droned on about the virtues of his publication, stating that he had come there merely as a friend, and to give the inhabitants of Ninemile a chance to buy a book which had already earned the approval of Dan O'Connor and the Earl of Jersey.

The genius and his mate watched this extraordinary drama through the window. They had kept up their courage with whisky and other stimulants, and now looked upon the whole affair as a wildly hilarious joke.

"By Gad! he's done him," said the genius as Macpherson went down, "done him in one hit. If he don't pay as a canvasser I'll take him to town and back him to fight Joe Goddard. Look out for yourself; don't you handle him!" he continued as the other approached the figure. "Leave him to me. As like as not, if you get fooling about him, he'll give you a smack in the snout that'll paralyse you."

So saying, he guided the automaton out of the office and into the street, and walked straight into — a policeman.

By a common impulse the genius and his mate at once ran rapidly away in different directions, and left the figure alone with the officer.

He was a fully ordained sergeant, by name Aloysius O'Grady; a squat, rosy little Irishman. He hated violent arrests and all that sort of thing, and had a faculty of persuading drunks and disorderlies and other fractious persons to "go quietly along with him", that was little short of marvellous. Excitable revellers, who were being carried along by their mates, struggling violently, would break away from their companions, and prance gaily along to the lock-up with the sergeant, whom, as likely as not, they would try to kiss on the way. Obstinate drunks who would do nothing but lie on the ground and kick their feet in the air, would get up like birds, serpent-charmed, and go with him to durance vile. As soon as he saw the canvasser, and noted his fixed, unearthly stare, and listened to his hoarse, unnatural voice, he knew what was the matter — it was a man in the horrors, a common enough spectacle at Ninemile. The sergeant resolved to decoy him into the lock-up, and accosted him in a friendly and free-and-easy way.

"Good day t'ye," he said.

"— Most magnificent volume ever published, jewelled in fourteen holes, working on a ruby roller, and in a glass case," said the book canvasser. "The likenesses of the historical personages are so natural that the book must not be left open on the table, or the mosquitoes will ruin it by stinging the faces of the portraits."

It then dawned on the sergeant that he was dealing with a book canvasser.

"Ah, sure," he said, "what's the use of tryin' to sell books at all, at all, folks does be peltin' them out into the street, and the nanny-goats lives on them these times. I sent the childher out to pick 'em up, and we have 'em at my place now — barrowloads of 'em. Come along wid me now, and I'll make you nice and comfortable for the night," and he laid his hand on the outstretched palm of the figure.

It was a fatal mistake. By so doing he set in motion the machinery which operated the figure's left arm, and it moved that limb in towards its body, and hugged the sergeant to its breast, with a vice-like grip. Then it started in a faltering, and uneven, but dogged way to walk towards the steep bank of the river, carrying the sergeant along with it.

"Immortal Saints!" gasped the sergeant, "he's squazin' the livin' breath out of me. Lave go now loike a dacent sowl, lave go. And oh, for the love of God, don't be shpakin' into my ear that way"; for the figure's mouth was pressed tight against the sergeant's ear, and its awful voice went through and through the little man's head, as it held forth about the volume. The sergeant struggled violently, and by so doing set some springs in motion, and the figure's right arm made terrific swipes in the air. A following of boys and loafers had collected by this time. "Bly me, how he does lash out!" was the admiring remark they made. But they didn't altogether like interfering, notwithstanding the sergeant's frantic appeals, and things would have gone hard with him had his subordinate Constable Dooley not appeared on the scene.

Dooley, better known to the town boys as the "Wombat", from his sleepy disposition, was a man of great strength. He had originally been quartered at Redfern, Sydney, and had fought many bitter battles with the Bondi Push, the Black Red Push, and the Surry Hills Push. After this the duty at Ninemile was child's play, and he never ran in less than two drunks at a time; it was beneath his dignity to be seen capturing a solitary inebriate. If they wouldn't come any other way, he would take them by the ankles and drag them after him. The townsfolk would have cheerfully backed him to arrest John L. Sullivan if necessary; and when he saw the sergeant in the grasp of an inebriate he bore down on the fray full of fight.

"I'll soon make him lave ye go, sergeant," he said, and he tried to catch hold of the figure's right arm, to put on the "police twist". Unfortunately at that exact moment the sergeant's struggles touched one of the springs in the creature's breast with more than usual force. With the suddenness and severity of a horse kick, it lashed out with its right hand, catching the redoubtable Dooley a regular thud on the jaw, and sending him to grass, as if he had been shot. For a few minutes he "lay as only dead men lie". They he got up bit by bit, and wandered off home to the police barracks and mentioned casually to his wife that John L. Sullivan had come to town, and had taken the sergeant away to drown him. After which, having given orders that if anybody called that visitor was to be told he had gone out of town fifteen miles to serve a summons on a man for not registering a dog, he locked himself into a cell for the rest of the day.

Meanwhile, the canvasser, still holding the sergeant tightly clutched to its breast, was marching straight towards the river. Something had disorganised the voice arrangements, and it was positively shrieking at the sergeant's ear, and, as it yelled, the little man yelled louder, "I don't want yer accursed book. Lave go of me, I say!" He beat with his fists on its face, and kicked at its shins without the slightest avail. A short, staggering rush, a wild shriek from the officer, and the two of them toppled over the steep bank and went souse into the bottomless depths of the Ninemile Creek.

That was the end of the whole matter. The genius and his mate returned to town hurriedly, and lay low, expecting to be indicted for murder. Constable Dooley drew up a report for the Chief of Police, which contained so many strange and unlikely statements that the department concluded the sergeant must have got drunk and drowned himself, and that Dooley saw him do it, but was too drunk to pull him out. Anyone unacquainted with Ninemile would have expected that a report of the occurrence would have reached the Sydney papers. As a matter of fact the storekeeper did think about writing a report, but decided that it was too much trouble. There was some idea of asking the Government to fish the two bodies out of the river, but about that time an agitation was started in Ninemile to have the Federal capital located there, and the other thing was forgotten. The genius drank himself to death; the "Wombat" became Sub-Inspector of Police; and a vague tradition about "a bloke who came up here in the horrors, and drownded poor old O'Grady", is the only memory that remains of that wonderful creation, the cast-iron canvasser.

As for the canvasser himself there is a rusted mass far down in the waters of the creek, and in its arms it holds a skeleton dressed in the rags of what was once a police uniform. And on calm nights the passers-by sometimes imagine they can hear, rising out of the green and solemn depths, a husky, slushy voice, like that of an iron man with mud and weeds and dishcloths in his throat, and that voice is still urging the skeleton to buy a book in monthly parts. But the canvasser's utterance is becoming weak and used up in these days, and it is only when the waters are low and the air is profoundly still that he can be heard at all.

# Bill and Jim
# Nearly Get Taken Down

"YOU SEE, it was this way," said Bill reflectively, as we sat on the rails of the horse yard, "me and Jim was down at Buckatowndown show with that jumpin' pony Jim has, and in the high jump our pony jumped seven foot, and they gave the prize to Spondulix that only jumped six foot ten. *You* know what these country shows are; a man can't get no sort of fair play at all. We asked the stooards why the prize was give to Spondulix, and they said because he jumped better style than the pony. So Jim he ups and whips the saddle and bridle off the pony, and he says to the cove at the jump, 'Put the bar up to seven foot six,' he says, and he rides the pony at it without saddle or bridle, and over he goes, never lays a toe on it, and Spondulix was frighted to come at it. And we offered to jump Spondulix for a hundred quid any time. And I went to the stooards and I offered to back the pony to run any horse on the ground two miles over as many fences as they could put up in the distance, and the bigger the better; and Jim, he offered to fight as many of the stooards as could get into a room with him. And even then they wouldn't give us the prize — a man can't ever get fair play at a country show. But what I wanted to tell you about was the way we almost got took down afterwards. By gum, it was a near thing!

"We went down from the show to the pub, and there was a lot o' toffs at the pub was bettin' Jim a pound here and a pound there that he wouldn't ride the pony at this fence and at that fence, and Jim picked up a few quid jumpin' 'em easy, for most of the fences weren't no more than six foot six high and, of course, that was like drinkin' tea to the pony. And at last one cove he points to a big palin' fence, and he says, 'I'll bet you a fiver your horse won't get over that one safely.' Well, of course, it was a fair-sized fence, being seven feet solid palin's, but we knew the pony could do it all right, and Jim wheels round to go at it. And just as he sails at it, I runs up to the fence and pulls myself up with my hands and looks over, and there was a great gully the other side a hundred feet deep and all rocks and stones. So I yelled out at Jim to stop, but it was too late, for he had set the pony going, and once that pony went at a fence you couldn't stop him with a block and tackle.

And the pony rose over the fence, and when Jim saw what was the other side, what do you think he did! Why, he turned the pony round in the air, and came back again to the same side he started from! My oath, it astonished those toffs. You see, they thought they would take us down about getting over safely, but they had to pay up because he went over the fence and back again as safe as a church. Did you say Jim must have been a good rider — well, not too bad, but that was nothin' to — hello, here comes the boss; I must be off. So long!"

THE MAN FOR THE JOB
The Bad One: "Wotto, Dad where are you going to stay this trip?"
The Simple One: "Oh, down at the Metropole, I suppose."
The Bad One: "Good, come and I'll take you down."

# *Bush Justice*

T HE town of Kiley's Crossing was not exactly a happy hunting ground for lawyers. The surrounding country was rugged and mountainous, the soil was poor, and the inhabitants of the district had plenty of ways of getting rid of their money without spending it in court.

Thus it came that for many years old Considine was the sole representative of his profession in the town. Like most country attorneys, he had forgotten what little law he ever knew, and, as his brand of law dated back to the very early days, he recognised that it would be a hopeless struggle to try and catch up with all the modern improvements. He just plodded along the best way that he could with the aid of a library consisting of a copy of the Crown Lands Acts, the *Miner's Handbook* and an aged mouse-eaten volume called *Ram on Facts* that he had picked up cheap at a sale on one of his visits to Sydney. He was an honourable old fellow, and people trusted him implicitly, and if he did now and then overlook a defect in the title to a piece of land — well, no one ever discovered it, as on the next dealing the title always came back to him again, and was, of course, duly investigated and accepted. But it was in court that he shone particularly. He always appeared before the police magistrate who visited Kiley's once a month. This magistrate had originally been a country storekeeper, and had been given this judicial position as a reward for political services. He knew less law than old Considine, but he was a fine, big, fat man, with a lot of dignity, and the simple country folk considered him a perfect champion of a magistrate. The fact was that he and old Considine knew every man, woman, and child in the district; they knew who could be relied on to tell the truth and whose ways were crooked and devious, and between them they dispensed a very fair brand of rough justice. If anyone came forward with an unjust claim, old Considine had one great case that he was supposed to have discovered in *Ram on Facts*, and which was dragged in to settle all sorts of points. This, as quoted by old Considine, was "the great case of Dunn v. Dockerty — the 'orse outside the 'ouse". What the 'orse did to the 'ouse or *vice versa* no one ever knew; doubts have been freely expressed whether there

INDIGNANT J.P. = LOOK HERE. I GIVE YOU ONE HOUR TO GET OUT OF THE TOWN.
PRISONER = IT'S IMPOSSIBLE. YOU KNOW I COULDN'T GET OUTSIDE EVEN THE CENTRE OF YOUR CITY IN THAT SHORT TIME.

MOLLIFIED J.P. = TRUE, GENTLEMEN, DON'T YOU THINK SOME OF US CITIZENS COULD RAISE A PURSE FOR THIS DESERVING YOUNG MAN?

A DIPLOMATIC ANSWER.

ever was such a case at all, and certainly, if it covered all the ground that old Considine stretched it over, it was a wondered decision.

However, genuine or not, whenever a swindle seemed likely to succeed, old Considine would rise to his feet and urbanely inform the bench that under the "well-known case of Dunn v. Dockerty — case that Your Worship of course knows — case of the 'orse outside the 'ouse", this claim must fail; and fail it accordingly did, to the promotion of justice and honesty. This satisfactory state of things had gone on for years, and might be going on yet only for the arrival at Kiley's of a young lawyer from Sydney, a terrible fellow, full of legal lore; he slept with digests and law reports; he openly ridiculed old Considine's opinions; he promoted discord and quarrels, with the result that on the first court day after his arrival, there was quite a little crop of cases, with a lawyer on each side — an unprecedented thing in the annals of Kiley's Crossing. In olden days one side or the other had gone to old Considine, and if he found that the man who came to him was in the wrong, he made him settle the case. If he was in the right, he promised to secure him the verdict, which he always did, with the assistance of *Ram on Facts* and "the 'orse outside the 'ouse". Now, however, all was changed. The new man struggled into court with an armful of books that simply struck terror to the heart of the P.M. as he took his seat on the bench. All the idle men of the district came into court to see how the old man would hold his own with the new arrival. It should be explained that the bush people look on a law case as a mere trial of wits between the lawyers and the witnesses and the bench; and the lawyer who can insult his opponent most in a given time is always the best in their eyes. They never take much notice of who wins the case, as that is supposed to rest on the decision of that foul fiend the law, whose vagaries no man may control nor understand. So, when the young lawyer got up and said he appeared for the plaintiff in the first case, and old Considine appeared for the defendant, there was a pleased sigh in court, and the audience sat back contentedly on their hard benches to view the forensic battle.

The case was simple enough. A calf belonging to the widow O'Brien had strayed into Mrs Rafferty's back yard and eaten a lot of washing off the line. There was ample proof. The calf had been seen by several people to run out of the yard with a half-swallowed shirt hanging out of its mouth. There was absolutely no defence, and in the old days the case would have been settled by payment of a few shillings, but here the young lawyer claimed damages for trespass to realty, damages for trover and conversion of personalty, damages for detinue, and a lot of other terrible things that no one had ever heard of. He had law books to back it all up, too. He opened the case in style, stating his authorities and defying his learned friend to contradict him, while the old P.M.

shuffled uneasily on the bench, and the reputation of old Considine in Kiley's Crossing hung trembling in the balance.

When the old man rose to speak he played a bold stroke. He said, patronisingly, that his youthful friend had, no doubt, stated the law correctly, but he seemed to have overlooked one little thing. When he was more experienced he would no doubt be more wary. (Sensation in court.) He relied upon a plea that his young friend had no doubt overlooked — that was that plea of "cause to show". "I rely upon that plea," he said, "and of course Your Worship knows the effect of that plea." Then he sat down amid the ill-suppressed admiration of the audience.

The young lawyer, confronted with this extraordinary manoeuvre, simply raged furiously. He asserted (which is quite true) that there is no such plea known to the law of this or any other country as an absolute defence to claim for a calf eating washing off a line, or to any other claim for that matter. He was proceeding to expound the law relating to trespass when the older man interrupted him.

"My learned friend says that he never heard of such a defence," he said, pityingly. "I think that I need hardly remind Your Worship that that very plea was successfully raised as a defence in the well known case of Dunn v. Dockerty, the case of the 'orse outside the 'ouse." "Yes," said the bench, anxious to display his legal knowledge, "that case — er — is reported in *Ram on Facts*, isn't it?" "Well, it is mentioned there, Your Worship," said the old man, "and I don't think that even my young friend's assurance will lead him so far as to question so old and well-affirmed a decision!" But his young friend's assurance did lead him that far, in fact, a good deal further. He quoted decisions by the score on every conceivable point, but after at least half an hour of spirited talk, the bench pityingly informed him that he had not quoted any cases bearing on the plea of "cause to show", and found a verdict for the defendant. The young man gave notice of appeal and of prohibitions and so forth, but his prestige was gone in Kiley's.

The audience filed out of court, freely expressing the opinion that he was a "regular fool of a bloke; old Considine stood him on his head proper with that plea of 'cause to show', and so help me goodness, he'd never even heard of it!"

# His Masterpiece

"GREENHIDE BILLY" was a stockman on a Clarence River cattle station and admittedly the biggest liar in the district. He had been for many years pioneering in the Northern Territory, the other side of the sundown — a regular "furthest-out man" — and this assured his reputation among station hands who award rank according to amount of experience. Young men who have always hung around the home localities, doing a job of shearing here or a turn at horse breaking there, look with reverence on the Riverine or Macquarie River shearers who come in with tales of runs where they have 300,000 acres of freehold land and shear 250,000 sheep, and these again pale their ineffectual fires before the glory of the Northern Territory man who has all comers on toast, because no one can contradict him or check his figures, except someone from the same locality. When two such meet, however, they are not fools enough to cut down quotations and spoil the market; no, they mutually lie in support of each other, and make all other bushmen feel mean and pitiful and inexperienced.

Sometimes a youngster would timidly ask Greenhide Billy about the (to him) *terra incognita*: "What sort of a place is it, Billy — how big are the properties? How many acres had you in the place you were on?"

"Acres be d —— d!" Billy would scornfully reply, "hear him talking about acres! D'ye think we were blanked cockatoo selectors? Out there we reckon country by the hundred miles. You orter say, 'How many thousand miles of country?' and then I'd understand you."

Furthermore, according to Billy, they reckoned the rainfall in the Territory by yards, not inches; he had seen blackfellows who could jump at least three inches higher than anyone else had ever seen a blackfellow jump, and evey bushman has seen or personally known a blackfellow who could jump over six feet. Billy had seen bigger droughts, better country, fatter cattle, faster horses, and cleverer dogs than any other man on the Clarence River. But one night when the rain was on the roof, and the river was rising with a moaning sound, and the men were gathered round the fire in the hut smoking and staring at the coals, Billy turned himself loose and gave us his masterpiece.

"I was drovin' with cattle from Mungrybanbone to old Corlett's station on the Buckatowndown River." (Billy always started his stories with some paralysing bush names.) "We had a thousand head of store cattle, wild mountain-bred wretches, they'd charge you on sight, and they were that handy with their horns they could skewer a mosquito. There was one or two one-eyed cattle among 'em, and you know how a one-eyed beast always keeps movin' away from the mob, pokin' away out to the edge of them so as they won't git on his blind side; and then by stirrin' about he keeps the others restless. They had been scared once or twice and stamped, and gave us all we could do to keep them together; and it was wet and dark and thundering, and it looked like a real bad night for us. It was my watch, and I was on one side of the cattle, like it might be here, with a small bit of a fire; and my mate, Barcoo Jim, he was right opposite on the other side of the cattle, and he had gone to sleep under a log. The rest of the men were in the camp fast asleep. Every now and again I'd get on my horse and prowl round the cattle quiet like, and they seemed to be settled down all right, and I was sitting by my fire holding my horse and drowsing, when all of a sudden a blessed possum ran out from some saplings and scratched up a little tree right alongside me. I was half asleep I suppose, and was startled, anyhow, never thinking what I was doing, I picked up a firestick out of the fire and flung it at the possum. Whoop! Before you could say 'Jack Robertson' that thousand head of cattle were on their feet, and they made one wild, headlong, mad rush right over the place where poor old Barcoo Jim was sleeping. There was no time to hunt up materials for the inquest; I had to keep those cattle together, so I sprang into the saddle, dashed the spurs into the old horse, dropped my head on his mane, and sent him as hard as he could leg it through the scrub to get the lead of the cattle and steady them. It was brigalow, and you know what that is. You know how the brigalow grows," continued Bill, "saplings about as thick as a man's arm, and that close together a dog can't open his mouth to bark in 'em. Well, those cattle swept through that scrub levelling it like as if it had been cleared for a railway line. They cleared a track a quarter of a mile wide, and smashed every stick, stump, and sapling on it. You could hear them roaring and their hoofs thundering and the scrub smashing three or four miles off. And where was I? I was racing parallel with the cattle with my head down on the horse's neck, letting him pick his way through the scrub in the pitchy darkness. This went on for about four miles, then the cattle began to get winded, and I dug into the old stock horse with the spurs, and got in front, and then began to crack the whip and sing out, so as to steady them a little; after a while they dropped slower and slower, and I kept the whip going. I got them all together in a patch of open country, and there I rode round and round 'em all night till daylight. And how I wasn't killed in the scrub, goodness only knows; for a man couldn't ride in the daylight where I did in the dark. The cattle were all knocked about — horns smashed, legs broken, ribs torn; but they were all there, every solitary head of 'em; and as soon as the daylight broke I took 'em back to the camp — that is, all that could travel, because a few broken-legged ones I had to leave."

Billy paused in his narrative. He knew that some suggestions would be made, by way of compromise, to tone down the awful strength of the yarn, and he prepared himself accordingly. His motto was, "No surrender"; he never abated one jot of his statements, and if anyone chose to remark on them, he made them warmer and stronger, and absolutely flattened out the intruder.

"That was a wonderful bit of ridin' you done, Billy," said one of the men at last, admiringly. "It's a wonder you wasn't killed. I s'pose your clothes was pretty well tore off your back with the scrub?"

"Never touched a twig." said Billy.

"Ah!" faltered the enquirer, "then no doubt you had a real ringin' good stock horse that could take you through a scrub like that full split in the dark, and not hit you against anything."

'No, he wasn't a good 'un," said Billy decisively, "he was the worst horse in the camp, and terrible awkward in the scrub he was, always fallin' down on his knees; and his neck was so short you could sit far back on him and pull his ears."

Here that interrogator retired hurt; he gave Billy best. Another took up the running after a pause.

"How did your mate get on, Billy? I s'pose he was trampled to a mummy!"

"No," said Billy, "he wasn't hurt a bit. I told you he was sleeping under the shelter of a little log. Well, when these cattle rushed they swept over that log a thousand strong; and every beast of that herd took the log in his stride and just missed landing on Barcoo Jimmy by about four inches. We saw the tracks where they had cleared him in the night — and fancy that, a thousand head of cattle to charge over a man in the dark and just miss him by a hair's breadth, as you might say!"

The men waited a while and smoked, to let this statement soak well into their systems; at last one rallied and had a final try to get a suggestion in somewhere.

"It's a wonder, then, Billy," he said, "that your mate didn't come after you and give you a hand to steady the cattle."

"Well, perhaps it was," said Billy, "only that there was a bigger wonder than that at the back of it."

"What was that?"

"My mate never woke all through it."

Then the men knocked the ashes out of their pipes and went to bed.

# Our Ambassador or Sharp Practice on the Darling

THERE is an old, furthest-out bushman who comes to Sydney once every year and always calls upon certain members of the staff of this paper. He seems to regard himself as an ambassador from the backblocks, and he lays down the law on all bush subjects in great style. He is a bearded, freckled old pirate, with a bald head. His hands are scarred with "Barcoo rot". There are not many parts of Australia that the ancient doesn't know; and to hear him chin off the old bush names is a perfect treat. He has a slightly Scotch accent, and he was at first suspected of being "Scotty the Wrinkler" in disguise, come "to take a rise" out of us. He always has a backblock story or two which he thinks would be highly suitable for publication. They never are. They mostly consist of yarns about the things which some renowned bullock driver said to his bullocks when he was fast in a river with a flood coming down. Or else he tells how, out in the far back country, the supplies got low and the only flour available was full of weevils and other livestock, and the storekeeper used to classify the flour according to the condition of the creeping things which inhabited it. The fatter the crawlers were, the better quality the flour was held to be so that "prime fat flour" sold at a considerable advance over that which was only in "store condition". His great idea is to have these stories illustrated, a process to which they do not lend themselves readily. But when he came to town this last time he was so genuinely distressed at none of his previous yarns having appeared that he was promised faithfully that "Sharp Practice on the Darling" should be published, even if the editor had to be knocked on the head.

"I've just come in from the Paroo," he said, "with cattle. And comin' down in the camp, the fellers was sayin' I ought to come and tell you some of the things as is happenin' up our way now. There's some tremenjus funny things in the bush, you know."

"Yes," we said. "What is the funniest thing that has happened lately?"

"Well," he replied, "we reckoned this was the funniest. We talked over a crowd of things in the camp, but we reckoned this was the best. It would make good pictures, too," he said, earnestly. "We call it sharp practice on the Darlin' River just now, and if a man has a fi' pun'-note he can't get past a public house with his life, you know. They'll get that fiver out of him, somehow. But there was a mate of mine that took 'em down all right" — and the old man chuckled at the remembrance.

"How did he take 'em down? Did he swallow the fiver and then cough it up after he got past the hotel?" we enquired.

"No," he said. "When he went to the pub, he had three fivers, and he gave the landlord two of 'em, and started a spree. So I come along and was havin' a drink with him, and he showed me the other fiver. 'I'm goin' to get away with this one,' says he. 'Does the publican know you've got it?' says I. 'Yes,' says he. 'Well, he'll have if off you somehow,' I says. 'There's no publican on the Darlin' River has let a man with five pounds get past him this seven years,' I says, 'and you ain't goin' to be the fust man to do it.' 'Won't I?' says he. 'You see, now, I'll get away with it all right.'

"So, when he'd about cut out his ten pounds, he slips down to the river one day, and takes the canoe, and paddles across, and makes off down the river to strike the coach road. The publican come out and 'Where's Hazard gone?' says he. Hazard was the name this mate of mine went by, and he was a tremenjus clever fellow — a real larrikin. 'I don't know,' says I, 'where he's gone.'

" 'Well,' says the publican, 'he owes me some money and I must have him back.' So he calls two chaps he had there, and he sends one to swim the river with a horse and go down the further side, and the other to go down the near side, and they was bound to have him that way. So Hazard, he was makin' down the river and he saw this cove cross over after him, and just then there was a steamer coming up the river. And he didn't want to go up the river, you know, but it was any port in a storm with him, so he runs to the bank and waves his swag, and the steamer sent a boat and took him off. And as he sent up past the public house he saw the landlord standing there, and he ran to the stern of the steamer and waves the fi-pun note at him. 'Ha! ha! old man,' he says, 'this is sharp practice on the Darling!' "

We agreed that this story would appeal strongly to bush readers. We also took notes of another narrative about a publican and a boozer. In this case the boozer had some pound notes and he let them blow out of his hand in the yard on a windy day, and then he, and the publican, and a retriever pup, were down on all fours together in the dirt grabbing at the notes as they blew about. The puppy secured the bulk of the capital. The old man pointed out that this would make a spirited illustration, and we promised to have a full-page drawing made of it when the artists had time. He went on to chat about things in general.

"About this Argentina scheme, now," he said, "you fellows in Sydney don't think that the bushmen are in earnest over that."

"Well, are they?" we enquired. "It doesn't look a very good game to leave this country and go to a strange place where they'll get potted like possums in the first revolution."

"Ah, well, they're in earnest about it," he said. "I'm not going myself, but there was six men at the last shed I was at that are going, and they have put down their stuff, too. It seems a pity, don't it, for them to go away. Fine strappin' young fellows as the sun ever shone on! But it's terrible hard to get a livin' these times," he said, "if you go shearing and get one shed it's all you'll do. And in the old times they was glad to get shearers. If it wasn't for the rabbits there'd be no work at all on a lot of the runs."

"Do the rabbits make much work?" we asked.

"Yes, they're too clever for men to keep out," he answered. "They burrows under the wire netting, and they can't be suffocated in their burrows nohow, 'cos they camp out under the saltbush these times. And they crosses the Murray River where it's a quarter of a mile wide."

"Oh, come! that's too stiff. You don't tell us the rabbits can swim a quarter of a mile?"

"In corse they don't," he said. "They burrows underneath it!"

After that we took him out and stood him a drink, and sent him on his way rejoicing.

# THE COMIC AUSTRALIAN

Registered at the G.P.O. for transmission by Post as a Newspaper.

Vol. I., No. 7.　　　NOVEMBER 18, 1911.　　　Price One Penny.

**THE OUTCASTS.**

Owing to the increased demand, it has been prophesied that the plebeian and ever-increasing bunny will succeed in ousting the aristocratic sheep.—News Item.

# The Merino Sheep

THE PROSPERITY of Australia is absolutely based on a beast — the merino sheep. If all the sheep in the country were to die, the big banks would collapse like card houses, the squatting securities, which are their backbone, being gone. Business would perish, and the money we owe to England would be as hopelessly lost to that nation as if we were a South American state. The sheep, and the sheep alone, keeps us going. On the back of this beneficent creature we all live. Knowing this, people have got the impression that the merino sheep is a gentle, bleating animal that gets its living without trouble to anybody, and comes up every year to be shorn with a pleased smile upon its amiable face. It is my purpose here, as one having experience, to exhibit the merino sheep in its true light, so that the public may know what kind of brute they are depending on.

And first let us give him what little credit is his due. No one can accuse him of being a ferocious animal. No one could ever say that a sheep attacked him without provocation, though there is an old bush story of a man who was discovered in the act of killing a neighbour's wether. "Hullo," said the neighbour. "What's this? Killing my sheep! What have you got to say for yourself?" "Yes," said the man, with an air of virtuous indignation. "I *am* killing your sheep. I'll kill *any* man's sheep that bites *me*!" But as a rule the merino refrains from using his teeth on people, and goes to work in another way.

The truth is that the merino sheep is a dangerous monomaniac, and his one idea is to ruin the man who owns him. With this object in view, he will display a talent for getting into trouble and a genius for dying that are almost incredible. If a mob of sheep see a bushfire closing round them, do they run away out of danger? Not at all; they rush round and round in a ring till the fire burns them up. If they are in a river bed, with a howling flood coming down, they will stubbornly refuse to cross three inches of water to save themselves. Dogs and men may bark and shriek, but the sheep won't move. They will wait there till the flood comes and drowns them all, and then their corpses go down the river on their backs with their feet in the air. A mob of sheep will crawl along a road slowly enough to exasperate a snail, but let a lamb get away from the mob in a bit of rough country, and a racehorse can't head him back again. If sheep are put into a big paddock with water in three corners of it, they will resolutely crowd into the fourth corner and die of thirst. When sheep are being counted out at the gate, if a scrap of bark be left on the ground in the gateway, they will refuse to step over it until dogs and men have sweated and toiled and sworn and "heeled 'em up", and "spoke to 'em", and fairly jammed them at it. Then the first one will gather courage, rush at the fancied obstacle, spring over it about six feet in the air and dart away. The next does exactly the same, but jumps a bit higher. Then comes a rush of them following one another in wild bounds like antelopes, until one "over-jumps himself" and alights on his head, a performance which nothing but a sheep could compass.

This frightens those still in the yard, and they stop running out, and the dogging and shrieking and hustling and tearing have to be gone through all over again. This on a red-hot day, mind you, with clouds of blinding dust about, with the yolk of wool irritating your eyes, and with, perhaps, three or four thousand sheep to put through . The delay throws out the man who is counting, and he forgets whether he left off at 45 or 95. The dogs, meanwhile, take the first chance to slip over the fence and hide in the shade somewhere. Then there are loud whistlings and oaths, and calls for Rover and Bluey, and at last a dirt-begrimed man jumps over the fence, unearths a dog and hauls him back to work by the ear. The dog sets to barking and heeling 'em up again, and pretends that he thoroughly enjoys it, but he is looking out all the time for another chance to "clear". And *this* time he won't be discovered in a hurry.

To return to our muttons. There is a well-authenticated story of a shipload of sheep being lost once, because an old ram jumped overboard into the ocean, and all the rest followed him. No doubt they did, and were proud to do it. A sheep won't go through an open gate on his own responsibility, but he would gladly and proudly follow another sheep through the red-hot portals of Hades: and it makes no difference whether the leader goes voluntarily or is hauled struggling and kicking and fighting every inch of the way. For pure, sodden stupidity there is no animal like the merino sheep. A lamb will follow a bullock dray drawn by sixteen bullocks and driven by a profane "colonial" with a whip, under the impression that this aggregate monstrosity is his mother. A ewe never knows her own lamb by sight, and apparently has no sense of colour. She can recognise her own lamb's voice half a mile off among a thousand other voices apparently exactly similar, but when she gets within five yards of her lamb she starts to smell all the lambs in reach, including the black ones, though her own may be a white lamb. The fiendish resemblance which one sheep bears to another is a great advantage to them in their struggles with their owners. It makes them more difficult to draft out of a strange flock, and much harder to tell when any are missing.

Concerning this resemblance between sheep, there is a story told of a fat old Murrumbidgee squatter who gave a big price for a famous ram called, say, Sir Oliver. He took a friend out one day to inspect Sir Oliver, and overhauled that animal with a most impressive air of sheep wisdom. "Look here," he said, "at the fineness of the wool. See the serrations in each thread of it. See the density of it. Look at the way his legs and belly are clothed — he's wool all over, that sheep. Grand animal, grand animal!" Then they went and had a drink, and the old squatter said. "Now, I'll show you the difference between a champion ram and a second-rater". So he caught a ram and pointed out his defects. "See here — not half the serrations that other sheep had. No density of fleece to speak of. Bare-bellied as a pig, compared with Sir Oliver. Not that this isn't a fair sheep, but he'd be dear at one-tenth Sir Oliver's price. By the way, Johnson" (to his overseer) "what ram *is* this?" "That, sir" replied the astounded functionary, "that's Sir Oliver, sir!" And so it was.

There is another kind of sheep in Australia, as great a curse in his own way as the merino — namely, the cross-bred or half-merino-half-Leicester animal. The cross-bred will get through, under or over any fence you like to put in front of him. He is never satisfied on his owner's run, but always thinks other people's runs must be better, so he sets off to explore. He will strike a course, say, south-east, and so long as the fit takes him he will keep going south-east through all obstacles, rivers, fences, growing crops — anything. The merino relies on passive resistance for his success; the cross-bred carries the war into the enemy's camp, and becomes a living curse to his owner day and night. Once there was a man who was induced in a weak moment to buy twenty cross-bred rams, and from that hour the hand of fate was upon him. They got into all the paddocks they shouldn't have been in. They scattered themselves all over the run promiscuously. They got into the cultivation paddock and the vegetable garden at their own sweet will. And then they took to roving. In a body they visited the neighbouring stations, and played havoc with the sheep all over the district. The wretched owner was constantly getting fiery letters from his neighbours: "Your . . . rams are here. Come and take them away at once", and he would have to go off nine or ten miles to drive them home. Any man who has tried to drive rams on a hot day knows what purgatory is. He was threatened with actions for trespass for scores of pounds damages every week. He tried shutting them up in the sheep yard. They got out and went back to the garden. Then he gaoled them in the calf pen. Out again and into a growing crop. Then he set a boy to watch them, but the boy went to sleep, and they were four miles away across country before he got on to their tracks. At length, when they happened accidentally to be at home on their owner's run, there came a huge flood. His sheep, mostly merinos, had plenty of time to get on to high ground and save their lives, but, of course, they didn't, and they were almost all drowned. The owner sat on a rise above the waste of waters and watched the dead animals go by. He was a ruined man. His hopes in life were gone. But he said, "Thank God, those rams are drowned, anyhow." Just as he spoke there was a splashing in the water, and the twenty rams solemnly swam ashore and ranged themselves in front of him. They were the only survivors of thousands of sheep. He broke down utterly, and was taken to an asylum for insane paupers. The cross-breds had fulfilled their destiny.

The cross-bred drives his owner out of his mind, but the merino ruins his man with greater celerity. Nothing on earth will kill cross-breds, while nothing will keep merinos alive. If they are put on dry saltbush country they die of drought. If they are put on damp, well-watered country they die of worms, fluke, and foot rot. They die in the wet seasons and they die in the dry ones. The hard, resentful look which you may notice on the faces of all bushmen comes from a long course of dealing with the merino sheep. It is the merino sheep which dominates the bush, and which gives to Australian literature its melancholy tinge, and its despairing pathos. The poems about dying boundary riders and lonely graves under mournful she-oaks are the direct outcome of the author's too close association with that soul-destroying animal, the merino sheep. A man who could write anything cheerful after a day in the drafting yards would be a freak of nature.

# In the Cattle Country

W E WERE going for a day in the cattle country, and also to vary it with a dash after dingoes. Nowadays there are not many cattle stations left in New South Wales, and there are fewer still where there are any dingoes; but there are still some bits of ragged country left where, even from the train, one can see the wary dingo slinking through the scrub and the wallaby skipping among the rocks

The trouble began at the homestead over the horses. Being drought time, one naturally thought that the horses would be poor and weak, and hardly able to gallop; instead of which they were all fed on maize and were fat and jumping out of their skins with animal spirits. The horse that I rode was a big bay with hair on his back and clipped underneath. He was introduced as a grandson of Musket, and the head stockman was enthusiastic about him.

"Man and boy," he said, "I've been ridin' horses for five and forty years, and this is the best horse I've ever ridden. There's no day too long for him. He can win a shearers' race, he can cut out cattle, and he can go through scrub like a wallaby."

"I suppose he won't hit me against a tree in the scrub, will he?"

"Oh, won't he just! He ain't afraid of a tree. He don't care where he goes."

"Does he pull much?"

"Well, if he gets woke-up like, he's a very hard horse to hold. We mostly ride him in a curb bit, but we put the snaffle on him for you. It was you wrote about the 'Man from Snowy River', wasn't it? Yes, well you ought to be able to ride him right enough."

This was a gay prospect for a man who had not ridden in scrub for ten years, and was never very expert at it at the best of times. Anyhow, I put a good face on it, and the grandson of Musket was brought forth ready saddled and bridled.

It was indeed a treat to ride such a horse — a great raking sixteen hand bay with black points, with enormous barrel and ribs, broad hips, and a shoulder laid right back till there seemed at least the length of an ordinary horse in front of the saddle. He was one of the examples of the old type of stockhorse — a horse with quality enough to run a

63

race, strength enough to pull a cart, and pluck enough to die galloping.

The head stockman did not come with us. He sent a sunburnt substitute who was well mounted, and who was the master of the dingo hounds, that is to say, he had with him a kangaroo slut, so narrow and wasp-waisted that she looked like an embodiment of hunger and speed, and a fierce-looking brown staghound, with a rough coat, and three sore feet, on which he limped alternately. But the genius of the party was Barney, the cattle dog, an aged dingo looking reprobate into whose face all the wisdom of centuries was crowded. It was understood that Barney would follow nothing but dingoes. Emus might frolic around him in flocks, kangaroos might leap affrighted from under his very nose, but nothing would turn Barney off a dingo.

The sunburnt stockman advised me, if I fell off or got lost, to sit still and not move about, as they were sure to find me again some time or other; and with this comforting advice we started. The young squatter who went with us was riding a station mare, well-bred, and a good mare in scrub, but running to weediness. The grandson of Musket strode out sleepily as a carthorse, lounging along as placidly as an old cow. The other two stockhorses fretted and fidgeted at their bits, but not so this veteran. He was waiting for the climax — the great critical moment when he would set the seal on his reputation by knocking me off against a tree and catching the dingo himself.

We rode through scrub and stringybark, over country consisting mostly of loose rocks up on end, and covered carefully from view by hop scrub, thickets of wattle, and the limbs of fallen trees. Sometimes we scrambled up hills, clinging round the horses' necks for fear we should slip over the tail. Other times we slid down mountains with the stones clattering round us, the horses blundering from rock to rock, and grazing our shins against the trees as they walked. We rode for hours without seeing any dingoes, or any cattle for that matter. Just mile after mile of worthless scrub and rock and wilderness: I was beginning to lose interest in the thing, and to believe that the dingoes were a myth, and to hope that after all the grandson of Musket wouldn't have the chance to destroy me against a tree, when all of a sudden, just as we were scrambling down the wickedest piece of rock and scrub in the world, the sunburnt stockman yelled out, "Hool 'im, hool 'im, hool 'im!" The sagacious Barney began to utter loud yelps of excitement; the greyhound and staghound flashed like arrows into the scrub; and the grandson of Musket took the bit in his teeth and tore through the timber, going as if he were on a racecourse, while the crash, crash, crash of the small scrub and fallen timber was punctuated by hairbreadth escapes — say twenty every second — from trees and saplings and overhanging branches. I never saw the dingo. I don't think anyone else did. We tore madly down the side of a range, arrived by some miracle at the foot of it, and there found ourselves face to face with a bottomless dry gully over which the grandson of Musket strode as if it were a crack in the earth; and then up, like rock wallabies, over the rocks and fallen stones on the opposite slope.

We had ridden about a mile. The two hounds had been out of sight from the very start. The feathery tail and the loud yelp of the sagacious Barney had been our guiding star — our oriflamme as it were — and now even Barney had disappeared. His yelping had suddenly ceased.

We managed to pull the horses up, and then everyone began to make excuses.

The sunburnt stockman started. "I was follerin' the kangaroo slut," he said, "and I see you two fellows makin' over here towards the left like, and I thought, of course, you must be on to the dingo, so I come over after you. That's how I come to lose the dorgs."

The young squatter followed suit. "I was following Ranji" [the deerhound] "but when I heard old Barney yelping I made across after him. And that bad clump of wattle delayed me a lot, and that's how I came to lose 'em."

Then they looked at me as if it was time for me to put in my explanation.

"How did you come to lose 'em?"

"Well," I said, "when I started of course I made sure of catching a dingo straight off, but I shaved the bark off so many saplings and knocked the limbs off so many trees with my head that my attention sort of wandered from the dogs. I wasn't following the dogs at all, it took me all my time to navigate this horse. That's how I came to lose the dogs."

The sunburnt stockman shook his head despondingly. "It's a pity," he said, "they're sure to catch him, in fact they've got him cot by now."

"Do you really think so?"

"Oh, certain," he said with a superior smile, "quite certain. They never miss a dorg, once they start him. Now, if we'd only kep' up with 'em, I'll bet you," he went on slowly and impressively "if we'd only kep' up with 'em, I'll bet you we would have found them now killin' him. After as good a run as a man could want! It's a great pity!"

It was indeed sad. Visions arose of the sagacious Barney and the shadow-like kangaroo slut engaged in the combat to the death with the dingo, who was dying silently, fighting to the last. I though sadly of all I was missing, for I had come all the way from Sydney to see a dingo killed, and now he was actually being killed, and I hadn't been able to keep up.

Here I happened to look over my shoulder and saw the sagacious Barney trying to dig a lizard out from under a fallen log, while the two hounds watched him with an air of grave interest.

"There they are," said I, "there's the dogs now."

The stockman wasn't a bit taken aback. "So they are," he said. "They must have come on-sighted. This time last year they missed a dingo just about the same way — just about here it was, too. It's only an accident like when they miss one, I tell you."

We had many another dash after Barney and his dingoes, and they all ended in the same way. The dogs dashed yelping out of sight, the horses tore through the scrub, the sunburnt stockman screamed encouragement from the rear, and the grandson of Musket swept through the timber over rocks and fallen logs, with the swoop of some great bird. After half a mile or so we would find ourselves left in the vast silence of the Australian bush, no dog nor dingo in sight; then we put in the time till the dogs came back, explaining to each other how it was that we had failed to keep up with them.

We didn't catch any dingoes. I saw one once in the distance and Barney was taken up and put on the scent; it was an anxious moment for me, because if Barney failed to howl and run on the scent, then that would have proved that I was a liar, and had not seen a dingo. Luckily for me Barney went nearly into hysterics when he came on the scent, and we had a glorious dash for a while; shortly after, we came on a dead yearling calf which the dingoes had killed. They had eaten the carcase almost out of the skin, leaving the empty skin like a discarded glove. The sunburnt stockman said that when they want to kill a calf they snap and bite at the heels of the mob till they start them racing, and as soon as a weak one falls to the rear, they snap at its hocks till they hamstring it; then they bite it to death.

The squatter produced a little bottle of strychnine and put some into the body of the calf. While he was doing this the sagacious Barney and the two hounds returned from their fruitless chase. Barney snuffed round the carcase for a while, then threw up his head and set off across the range at a businesslike trot.

"Look at him," said the stockman. "He's on to 'em! He's trailin' 'em! There's been a lot round that calf, and he'll be on to 'em in a minute! Be ready now! Be ready! That's the way he always goes when he's trailin' 'em!"

My heart beat high with excitement. I gripped the grandson of Musket by the head and peered through the dense timber to see if I could risk a hundred yards of safe going, so that I might see a little of the hunt before I was killed. I expected a summons to death at any moment.

With intense excitement we watched Barney pause on the top of the rocks and snuff the air, irresolute; then he trotted on for some distance and wagged his tail, evidently having found what he wanted. There was a pool of water there and he lay down in it; he had not been after

INCONSIDERATE

The Boss: " 'Ere, be careful. Yer'll be fallin' in there and
getin' drowned. Do yer want us ter go right down
ter the creek fer our water? "

dingoes at all; having slaked his thirst, he trotted back and began to eat the poisoned calf. I suggested that in reward for having sold us like that, he should be allowed to eat as much of it as he wanted, but his owner explained that there had been dingoes drinking at the waterhole and Barney had gone there to see if any were planted near there. No matter what happened, you couldn't shake his faith in Barney.

After this contretemps we lost interest in the dingoes and went to look for cattle. We found a few poor starving relics, eating the scrub which was cut down for them from day to day. When they first came on the place, they were so wild that the sight of a man would set them galloping in all directions, and now, as soon as they heard an axe they would come crowding down to it.

Cattle are going to be worth phenomenal money after the drought. Judging by what we saw in the bush, next year's export of frozen meat will be mostly frozen bone dust.

The hounds caught a few kangaroos during the day, and the shades of night saw us returning to the station with horses, dogs, and men all pretty tired, and no result in the shape of dingoes. But that wasn't Barney's fault. As his owner said, "If we'd only have been able to have kept up, he would have got a lot of 'em."

# White-When-He's-Wanted

BUCKALONG was a big freehold of some 80,000 acres, belonging to an absentee syndicate, and therefore run in most niggardly style. There was a manager on two hundred pounds a year, Sandy McGregor to wit — a hard-headed old Scotchman known as "four-eyed McGregor", because he wore spectacles. For assistants, he had half-a-dozen of us — jackaroos and colonial experiencers — who got nothing a year, and earned it. We had, in most instances, paid premiums to learn the noble art of squatting, which now appears to me hardly worth studying, for so much depends on luck that a man with a head as long as a horse's has little better chance than the fool just imported. Besides the manager and the jackaroos, there were a few boundary riders to prowl round the fences of the vast paddocks. This constituted the whole station staff.

Buckalong was on one of the main routes by which stock were taken to market, or from the plains to the tablelands, and *vice versa*. Great mobs of travelling sheep constantly passed through the run, eating up the grass and vexing the soul of the manager. By law sheep must travel six miles per day, and they must keep within half a mile of the road. Of course, we kept all the grass near the road eaten bare, to discourage travellers from coming that way. Such hapless wretches as did venture through Buckalong used to try hard to stray from the road and pick up a feed, but old Sandy was always ready for them, and would have them dogged right through the run. This bred feuds, and bad language, and personal combats between us and the drovers, whom we looked upon as natural enemies. Then the men who came through with mobs of cattle used to pull down the paddock fences at night, and slip the cattle in for refreshments; but old Sandy often turned out at 2 or 3 a.m. to catch a big mob of bullocks in the horse paddock, and then off they went to Buckalong pound. The drovers, as in duty bound, attributed the trespass to accident-broken rails, and so on — and sometimes they tried to rescue the cattle, which again bred strife and police court summonses.

Besides having a particular aversion to drovers, old McGregor had a general "down" on the young "colonials", whom he comprehensively described as a "feckless, horse-dealin', horse-stealin', crawlin' lot o' wretches". According to him, a native would sooner work a horse to death than work for a living, any day. He hated any man who wanted to sell him a horse. "As ah walk the street," he used to say, "the folk disna stawp me to buy claes nor shoon, an' wheerfore should they stawp me to buy horses? It's 'Mister McGregor, will ye purrchase a horrse?' Let them wait till I ask them to come wi' theer horrses."

Such being his views on horseflesh and drovers, we felt no little excitement when one Sunday, at dinner, the cook came in to say there was a "drover chap outside wanted the boss to come and have a look at a horse". McGregor simmered awhile, and muttered something about the "Sawbath day"; but at last he went out, and we filed after him to see the fun.

The drover stood by the side of his horse, beneath the acacia trees in the yard. He had a big scar on his face, apparently the result of collision with a tree; and seemed poverty-sticken enough to disarm hostility. Obviously, he was "down on his luck". He looked very thin and sickly, with clothes ragged and boots broken. Had it not been for that indefinable self-reliant look which drovers — the Ishmaels of the bush — always acquire, one might have taken him for a swagman. His horse was in much the same plight. A ragged, unkempt pony, pitifully poor and very footsore — at first sight, an absolute "moke", but a second glance showed colossal round ribs, square hips, and a great length of rein, the rest hidden beneath a wealth of loose hair. He looked like "a good journey horse", possibly something better.

We gathered round while McGregor questioned the drover. The man was monosyllabic to a degree, as real bushmen generally are. It is only the rowdy and the town-bushy that is fluent of speech.

"Good morning," said McGregor.

"Mornin', boss," said the drover, shortly.

"Is this the horrse ye have for sale?"

"Yes."

"Aye", and McGregor looked at the pony with a businesslike don't-think-much-of-him air; ran his hand lightly over the hard legs and opened the passive creature's mouth. "H'm," he said. Then he turned to the drover. "Ye seem a bit oot o' luck. Ye're thin, like. What's been the matter?"

"Been sick with fever — Queensland fever. Just come through from the north. Been out on the Diamantina last."

"Aye. I was there mysel'," said McGregor. "Have ye the fever on ye still?"

"Yes — goin' home to get rid of it."

It should be explained that a man can only get Queensland fever in a malarial district, but he can carry it with him wherever he goes. If he stays, it will sap all his strength and pull him to pieces; if he moves to a better climate, the malady moves with him, leaving him only by degrees, and coming back at regular intervals to rack, shake, burn, and sweat its victim. Queensland fever will pull a man down from fifteen stone to nine stone faster, and with greater certainty, than any system of dosing yet invented. Gradually it wears itself out, often wearing its patient out at the same time. McGregor had been through the experience, and there was a slight change in his voice as he went on with the palaver.

"Where are ye makin' for the noo?"

"Monaro — my people live in Monaro."

"How will ye get to Monaro if ye sell the horrse?"

"Coach and rail. Too sick to care about ridin'," said the drover, while a wan smile flitted over his yellow-grey features. "I've rode him far enough. I've rode that horse a thousand miles. I wouldn't sell him, only I'm a bit hard up. Sellin' him now to get the money to go home."

"How old is he?"

"Seven."

"Is he a good horse on a camp?" asked McGregor.

"No better camp horse in Queensland," said the drover. "You can chuck the reins on his neck, an' he'll cut out a beast by himself."

McGregor's action in this matter puzzled us. We spent our time crawling after sheep, and a camp horse would be about as much use to us as side pockets to a pig. We had expected Sandy to rush the fellow off the place at once, and we couldn't understand how it was that he took so much interest in him. Perhaps the fever-racked drover and the old camp horse appealed to him in a way to us incomprehensible. We had never been on the Queensland cattle camps, nor shaken and shivered with the fever, nor lived the roving life of the overlanders. McGregor had done all this, and his heart (I can see it all now) went out to the man who brought the old days back to him.

"Ah, weel," he said, "we hae'na much use for a camp horrse here, ye ken; wi'oot some of these lads wad like to try theer han' cutttin' oot the milkers' cawves frae their mithers." And the old Man laughed contemptuously, while we felt humbled and depraved in the eyes of the man from far back. "An' what'll ye be wantin' for him?" asked McGregor.

"Reckon he's worth fifteen notes," said the drover.

This fairly staggered us. Our estimates had varied between thirty shillings and a fiver. We thought the negotiations would close abruptly, but McGregor, after a little more examination, agreed to give the price, provided the saddle and bridle, both grand specimens of ancient art, were given in. This was agreed to, and the drover was sent off to get his meals in the hut before leaving by the coach.

"The mon is verra hard up, an it's a sair thing that Queensland fever," was the only remark that McGregor made. But we knew that there was a soft spot in his heart somewhere.

And so, next morning, the drover got a crisp-looking cheque and departed by coach. He said no word while the cheque was being written, but, as he was going away, the horse happened to be in the yard, and he went over to the old comrade that had carried him so many miles and laid a hand on his neck. "He ain't much to look at," said the drover, speaking slowly and awkwardly, "but he's white, when he's wanted." And just before the coach rattled off, the man of few words lent down from the box and nodded impressively, and repeated, "Yes, he's white when he's wanted."

We didn't trouble to give the new horse a name. Station horses are generally called after the man from whom they are bought. "Tom Devine", "the Regan mare", "Black McCarthy", and "Bay McCarthy" were amongst the appellations of our horses at that time. As we didn't know the drover's name, we simply called the animal "the new horse" until a still newer horse was one day acquired. Then, one of the hands being told to take the new horse, said "D'yer mean the *new* new horse or the *old* 'new horse'?" "No," said the boss, "not the new horse — that bay horse we bought from the drover. The one he said was white when he was wanted."

And so, by degrees, the animal came to be referred to as the horse that's white when he's wanted, and at last settled down to the definite name of "White-when-he's-wanted".

White-when-he's-wanted didn't seem much of an acquisition. He was sent out to do slavery for Greenhide Billy, a boundary rider who plumed himself on having once been a cattle man. After a week's experience of "White", Billy came in to the homestead disgusted — the pony was so lazy that he had to build a fire under him to get him to move, and so rough that it would make a man's nose bleed to ride him more than a mile. "The boss must have been off his head to give fifteen notes for such a cow."

McGregor heard this complaint. "Verra weel, Mr Billy," said he, hotly, "ye can just tak' one of the young horrses in yon paddock, an' if he bucks wi' ye, an' kills ye, it's yer ain fault. Ye're a cattle man — so ye say — dommed if ah believe it. Ah believe ye're a dairy farmin' body frae Illawarra. Ye don't know neither horrse nor cattle. Mony's the time ye never rode buck jumpers, Mr Billy," and with this parting shot the old man turned into the house, and White-when-he's-wanted came back to the head station.

For a while he was a sort of pariah. He used to yard the horses, fetch up the cows, and hunt travelling sheep through the run. He really was lazy and rough, and we all decided that Billy's opinion of him was

71

correct, until the day came to make one of our periodical raids on the wild horses in the hills at the back of the run. Every now and again we formed parties to run in some of these animals, and, after nearly galloping to death half a dozen good horses, we would capture three or four brumbies, and bring them in triumph to the homestead. These we would break in, and by the time they had thrown half the crack riders on the station, broken all the bridles, rolled on all the saddles and kicked all the dogs, they would be marketable (and no great bargains) at about thirty shillings a head.

Yet there is no sport in the world to be mentioned in the same volume as "running horses", and we were very keen on it. All the crack nags were got as fit as possible, and fed up beforehand, and on this particular occasion White-when-he's-wanted, being in good trim, was given a week's hard feed and lent to a harum-scarum fellow from the upper Murray who happened to be working in a survey camp on the run. How he did open our eyes. He ran the mob from hill to hill, from range to range, across open country and back again to the hills, over flats and gullies, through hop scrub and stringybark ridges; and all the time White-when-he's-wanted was on the wing of the mob, pulling double. The mares and foals dropped out, then the colts and young stock pulled up deadbeat, and only the seasoned veterans of the mob were left. Most of our horses caved in altogether; one or two were kept in the hunt by judicious nursing and shirking the work, but White-when-he's-wanted was with the quarry from end to end of the run, doing double his share; and at the finish, when a chance offered to wheel them into the trap yard, he simply smothered them for pace and slowed them into the wings before they knew where they were. Such a capture had not fallen to our lot for many a day, and the fame of White-when-he's-wanted was speedily noised abroad.

He was always fit for work, always hungry, always ready to lie down and roll, and always lazy. But when he heard the rush of the brumbies' feet in the scrub, he became frantic with excitement. He could race over the roughest ground without misplacing a hoof or altering his stride, and he could sail over fallen timber and across gullies like a kangaroo. Nearly every Sunday we were after the brumbies until they got as lean as greyhounds and as cunning as policemen. We were always ready to back White-when-he's-wanted to run down, single handed, any animal in the bush that we liked to put him after — wild horses, wild cattle, kangaroos, emus, dingoes, kangaroo rats — we barred nothing, for, if he couldn't beat them for pace, he would outlast them.

And then one day he disappeared from the paddock, and we never saw him again. We knew there were plenty of men in the district who would steal him, but, as we knew also that there were plenty more who would "inform" for a pound or two, we were sure that it could not have been the local "talent" who had taken him. We offered good rewards and set some of the right sort to work, but we heard nothing of him for about a year.

Then the surveyor's assistant turned up again after a trip to the interior. He told us the usual string of backblock lies, and then wound up by saying that out on the very fringe of settlement he had met an old acquaintance.

"Who was that?"

"Why, that little bay horse that I rode after the brumbies that time. The one you called White-when-he's-wanted."

"The deuce you did! Are you sure? Who had him?"

"Sure? I'd swear to him anywhere. A little drover fellow had him. A little fellow, with a big scar across his forehead. Came from Monaro way, somewhere. He said he bought the horse from you for fifteen notes."

And then there was a chorus about the thief getting seven years.

But he hasn't so far, and, as the Queen's warrant doesn't run much out west of Boulia, it is not at all likely that any of us will ever see the drover again, or will ever again cross the back of "White-when-he's-wanted."

# The History of a Jackaroo in Five Letters

## NUMBER 1

### LETTER FROM JOSCELYN DE GREENE, OF WILTSHIRE, ENGLAND, TO COLLEGE FRIEND

DEAR GUS,

The Governor has fixed things up for me at last. I am not to go to India, but to Australia. It seems the Governor met some old Australian swell named Moneygrub at a dinner in the City. He has thousands of acres of land and herds of sheep, and I am to go out and learn the business of sheep raising. Of course it is not quite the same as going to India; but some really decent people do go out to Australia sometimes, I am told, and I expect it won't be so bad. In India one generally goes into the Civil Service, nothing to do and lots of niggers to wait on you but the Australian Civil Service no fellow can well go into — it is awful low business, I hear. I have been going in for gun and revolver practice so as to be able to hold my own against the savages and the serpents in the woods of Australia. Mr Moneygrub says there isn't much fighting with the savages nowadays; but, he says, the Union shearers will give me all the fight I want. What is a Union shearer, I wonder? My mother has ordered an extra large artist's umbrella for me to take with me for fear of sunstroke, and I can hold it over me while watching the flocks. She didn't half like my going until Mr Moneygrub said that they always dressed for dinner at the head station, and that a Church of England clergyman visits there twice a month. I am only to pay a premium of £500 for the experience, and Mr Moneygrub says I'll be able to make that out of scalps in my spare time. He says there is a Government reward for scalps. I don't mind a brush with the savages, but if he thinks I'm going to scalp my enemies he is mistaken. Anyhow, I sail next week, so no more from yours, outward bound,

Joscelyn de Greene.

# THE COMIC AUSTRALIAN

Registered at the G.P.O. for transmission by Post as a Newspaper.

## A JOURNAL OF FACT, FUN, AND FICTION.

VOL. 2, NO. 47.     AUGUST 20, 1912.     Price, One Penny.

## CHOLLY 'ROO HUNTING.

"By Jove, chappie, huwwy up. Heah comes a wild kangawoo."

'Roo: What price me for the next Olympiad?"

"Shoo!"

"Toot-too, Boys."

CHOLLY 'ROO HUNTING

1. " By Jove, chappie, huwwy up. Heah comes a wild kangawoo."
2. " Roo: What price me for the next Olympiad? "
3. " Shoo! "
4. " Toot-toot, Boys. "

## NUMBER 2

### LETTER FROM MONEYGRUB AND CO., LONDON, TO THE MANAGER OF THE COMPANY'S DRYBONE STATION, PAROO RIVER, AUSTRALIA

DEAR SIR,

 We beg to advise you of having made arrangements to take a young gentleman named Greene as colonial experiencer, and he will be consigned to you by the next boat. His premium is £500, and you will please deal with him in the usual way. Let us know when you have vacancies for any more colonial experiencers, as several are now asking about it, and the premiums are forthcoming. You are on no account to employ Union shearers this year; and you must cut expenses as low as you can. Would it not be feasible to work the station with the colonial experience men and Chinese labour? &c., &c., &c.

## NUMBER 3

### LETTER FROM MR ROBERT SALTBUSH, OF FRYING PAN STATION, TO A FRIEND

DEAR BILLY,

 Those fellows over at Drybone station have been at it again. You know it joins us, and old Moneygrub, who lives in London, sends out an English bloke every now and again to be a jackaroo. He gets £500 premium for each one, and the manager puts the jackaroo to boundary ride a tremendous great paddock at the back of the run, and he gives him a week's rations and tells him never to go through a gate, because so long as he only gets lost in the paddock he can always be found somehow, but if he gets out of the paddock, Lord knows whether he'd ever be seen again. And there these poor English devils are, riding round the fences and getting lost and not seeing a soul until they go near mad from loneliness; and then they run away at last, and old Macgregor, the manager, he makes a great fuss and goes after them with a whip, but he takes care to have a stockman pick their tracks up and take them to the nearest township, and then they go on the spree and never come back, and old Moneygrub collars the £500 and sends out another jackaroo. It's a great game. The last one they had was a fellow called Greene. They had him at the head station for a while, letting him get pitched off the station horses. He said: "They're awfully beastly horses in this country, by Jove; they're not content with throwing you off, but they'd kick you afterwards if you don't be careful." When they got full up of him at the head station they sent him out to the big paddock to an old hut full of fleas, and left him there with his tucker and two old screws of horses. The horses, of course, gave him the slip, and he got lost for two days looking for them, and his meat was gone bad when he got home. He killed a sheep for tucker, and how do you think he killed it? He shot it! It was a ram, too, one of Moneygrub's best rams, and there will be the deuce to pay when they find out. About the fourth day a swagman turned up, and he gave the swaggie a gold watch chain to show him the way to the nearest town, and he is there now — on the spree, I believe. He had a fine throat for whisky, anyhow, and the hot climate has started him in earnest. Before he left the hut and the fleas, he got a piece of raddle and wrote on the door: "Hell. S.R.O.", whatever that means. I think it must be some sort of joke. The brown colt I got from Ginger is a clinker, a terror to kick, but real fast. He takes a lot of rubbing out for half a mile, &c., &c., &c.

## NUMBER 4

### LETTER FROM SANDY MACGREGOR, MANAGER OF DRYBONE STATION, TO MESSRS MONEYGRUB & CO., LONDON

DEAR SIRS,
	I regret to have to inform you that the young gentleman, Mr Greene, whom you sent out, has seen fit to leave his employment and go away to the township. No doubt he found the work somewhat rougher than he had been used to, but if young gentlemen are sent out here to get experience they must expect to rough it like other bushmen. I hope you will notify his friends of the fact: and if you have applications for any more colonial experiencers we now have a vacancy for one. There is great trouble this year over the shearing, and a lot of grass will be burnt unless some settlement is arrived at. &c., &c., &c.

## NUMBER 5

### EXTRACT FROM EVIDENCE OF SENIOR CONSTABLE RAFFERTY, TAKEN AT AN INQUEST BEFORE LUSHINGTON, P.M. FOR THE NORTH-EAST BY SOUTH PAROO DISTRICT, AND A JURY

I am a senior constable, stationed at Walloopna beyant. On the 5th instant, I received information that a man was in the horrors at Flanagan's hotel. I went down and saw the man, whom I recognise as the deceased. He was in the horrors: he was very bad. He had taken all his clothes off, and was hiding in a fowl house to get away from the devils which were after him. I went to arrest him, but he avoided me, and escaped over a paling fence on to the Queensland side of the border, where I had no power to arrest him. He was foaming at the mouth and acting like a madman. He had been on the spree for several days. From enquiries made, I believe his name to be Greene, and that he had lately left the employment of Mr Macgregor, at Drybone. He was found dead on the roadside by the carries coming into Walloopna. He had evidently wandered away from the township, and died from the effects of the sun and the drink.

Verdict of jury: "That deceased came to his death by sunstroke and exposure during a fit of delirium tremens caused by excessive drinking. No blame attached to anybody." Curator of intestate estates advertises for next of kin of J. Greene, and nobody comes forward. Curtain!

# The Oracle in the Barber's Shop

"YOU'RE NEXT!" called the Barber, as the Oracle put his head in the saloon on Monday morning. "Won't keep you a minute." The Oracle stepped in to find, as usual, six men waiting to be shaved, each with a chin on him as bristly as the barrel of a musical box.

There may have been at some time in some country a barber who told the truth about how long the unshaven customer would have to wait; but, if so, he is now in Heaven, with the only politician who ever told the truth about the prospects of his party.

But the Oracle was in no particular hurry, and had not believed the Barber when the latter told him he was "next". Nobody ever takes a barber's word in a matter of that sort, without seeing that the saloon is empty.

"It's a bit awkward in this business," said the Barber. "Can't help keeping people waiting on Saturdays and Mondays. Can't put on extra hands, because all the shops want 'em at the same time and if there were enough to go all round on Saturdays and Mondays, three-fourths of them would be unemployed all the rest of the week, as a good many are now."

"But I don't find customers growl much," proceeded the Tonsorial Artist, as he scraped some more bristles off the neck of the gentleman in the chair. "I don't know how women would stand waiting in a shaving saloon. It's a good job they don't have beards."

"I suppose," whispered the Oracle to the Thin Man seated next to him, and who looked as if he had swallowed a bird cage, and the wire were growing out of his chin, "I suppose you know why it is that women don't have beards?"

"I should imagine," said the Thin Man with the porcupine bristles, "that it is in accord with the natural law under which the male animal is the most beautiful. Compare the peacock with the peahen."

"Just so," said the Oracle, "one never hears of a peacock being discounted, and subsequently dishonoured, but it is a thing that frequently happens in the case of a P.N."

"Observe," went on the Thin Man, "the noble mane of the lion as compared — I should say contrasted — with the smooth neck of the lioness."

"Exactly," said the Oracle. "Then there is the Lyre Bird and the Bird of Paradise; how beautiful are the male birds! But the case of the Queen Bee shows that the law of male superiority is not universal, as is commonly supposed. And the reason that women have no beards has no bearing on the question of sex superiority at all!"

"No?" queried the Thin Man.

"Certainly not," said the Oracle. "The reason that women have no beards is that the Creator was aware that no woman could possibly keep her chin still long enough to admit of her being shaved without being in imminent danger of having her throat cut. That is why men have beards, and women do not. Dowie has a fine beard."

"Yes," said the Thin Man. "Strange form of religion he has, isn't it?"

"There is nothing very new about it," said the Oracle. "Faith-healing is as old as the hills, and has caused the deaths of tens of thousands of people at various periods of the world's history. Oliver Cromwell was a great believer in faith. What did he say at the battle of Marston Moor? 'Put your faith in the Lord and don't forget to keep the powder dry!' Voltaire was also very strong on faith."

"Voltaire?" said the Thin Man, with the fencing-wire whiskers. "Why, he was an atheist!"

"It is a common idea," said the Oracle, "but it is just as erroneous, as it is common. When charged with atheism, Voltaire said he was not an atheist, or an agnostic, but he went so far in the opposite direction that he was profoundly superstitious. 'So far from believing in nothing,' he said, 'I can believe in witchcraft and am confident that with incantations (and arsenic) it is possible to poison a flock of sheep!'"

"Next!" called the Barber, and Thin Man went into the chair.

"If I had a stubbly beard like that," said the Oracle to the Fat Man who had moved along the form, and came nearer, when the Thin Man took the chair. "If I had a beard like that, I think I would run the lawn mower over it before I had the impudence to bring it into a barber's shop to be shaved off for threepence."

"Perhaps he doesn't own a lawn mower," suggested the Fat Man.

"Then he should use a keyhole saw or a jack plane," said the Oracle, "or he should borrow a scythe blade. It isn't shaving at all; it is harvesting a heavy crop, with plenty of thistles and cobbler's pegs among the wheat!"

"What's your opinion," asked the Fat Man, "about this retrenchment scheme? Pretty rough to make the civil servants pay for the extravagance of the Government, ain't it?"

"It is," said the Oracle. "The trouble is they don't begin at the right end."

"That's it; they should cut down the big screws," said the Fat Man.

"I didn't mean that," said the Oracle. "What we want is a sliding scale of payment for Ministers and members. Of course, they don't cause the drought; but as they always take credit for a good season, we might as well blame them for a bad one, just to even things up a bit. If I had my way I'd have payment by results. The Treasurer shouldn't be allowed to use any revenue to the extent of a cab fare until the money was voted by Parliament, and Ministers' and members' salaries should be put on the Estimates, and be liable to alteration every year. There never was a Treasurer anywhere who even anticipated a deficit, and I don't remember one in this country that ever had a surplus of more than about half a crown, and he only got that by charging a million of current expenses to loan account. What we want is to make the Treasurer run the finances so that the balance at the end of the year will be something like what he prophesied at the start."

"How on earth could you do that?" asked the Fat Man.

"Wait till I tell yer," proceeded the Oracle. "There are always a lot of people in favour of retrenching somebody else; but I'd make it compulsory for the politicians to retrench themselves."

"Well, they've done that now," said the Fat Man.

"They've reduced the numbers," said the Oracle, "but that's no use, except that it saves a good bit of gas. The saving in salaries will only be fooled away in some other direction. This is what I'd do. When the Treasurer made his financial statement, and gave his forecast, I'd make it a matter of direct personal interest to him and every other politician to carry out the pledges given in the forecast. If the surplus for the year was 10 per cent below the estimate, the Parliamentary salaries, from the Premier's down to the Boghollow representative's, should be reduced 20 per cent, and if the surplus was 10 per cent above the estimate, their salaries should be raised 5 per cent. And no statement at the end of a financial year should be admitted as correct unless signed by the Premier, and countersigned by the Leader of the Opposition, who, when there was a surplus, could count over the amount of it in hard cash. Suppose you were a member of Parliament —"

"I am," interrupted the Fat Man.

"Oh, you are, are yer? Well, you've got a good job, and I hope you won't be one of the 35 unfortunates. Well, the amount of your screw should depend on the correctness of the Treasurer's Estimates. When there was a deficit, you'd lose 10 per cent, if the deficit was 10 per cent, and when there was a surplus of the same amount, you'd gain 5 per cent. You'd take jolly fine care that O'Sullivan didn't fool too much money away in some other chap's electorate, and the other chap would have his weather eye on O'Sullivan's beneficence in your back yard, and you'd all see that the Treasurer didn't waste any money on statues of Australia Making Faces at the Pawnshop. My word, when Parliament is the first place to be retrenched in case of a deficit, you can take my tip there'll always be a surplus!"

"Next!" called the Barber.

And the Oracle took the chair.

# *Preparing for Premiers*

## A SKETCH AT THE TIME OF
## QUEEN VICTORIA'S JUBILEE

*SCENE*: Office of High Official in charge of Colonial affairs in London. High Official discovered glaring at table covered with lists of visiting potentates, programmes of amusements, lists of precedence, cablegrams, &c., &c. A waste-paper basket full of K.C.M.G. ribbons and orders stands by the table. On the table a handbag full of Privy Councillorships. High Official rings bell angrily. To him enters subordinate official, the Honourable Somebody, a very tired-looking youth.

HIGH OFFICIAL: "Look here, this is a nice state of things. I'm only just back from Monte Carlo, and I've got to set to work and clear up all this business. Now, have you got a list of the people we are responsible for?"

TIRED YOUTH: "Ya-a-as."

HIGH OFFICIAL: "Well, who *is* there? There's the Indian Viceroy, of course, and the Premier of Canada — we know all about *them*. And then there's the chappie from China, my brother-in-law, *he's* all right. But what about these Australian brutes? How many are there? Two, I suppose — Premier of South Australia and Premier of North Australia — eh? there must be a North Australia if there's a South Australia! Where's your list — how many are there?"

TIRED YOUTH: "There's seven."

HIGH OFFICIAL: "*Seven*! Good God, are the whole population Premiers over there? There's not seven places for them to be Premiers of! You must have made a mistake. Get the map!" (*They get the map and pore over it discontentedly.*)

HIGH OFFICIAL (*triumphantly*): "There you are! What did I tell you! There's only five colonies, even if each place has a Premier, which I don't believe. There's Queensland, New South Wales, Victoria, South

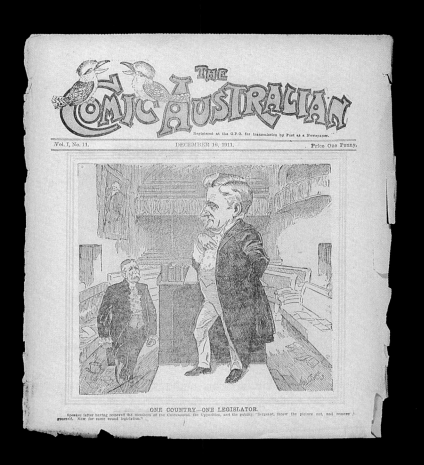

ONE COUNTRY – ONE LEGISLATOR
Speaker ( after having removed the members of the Government,
the Opposition and the public ) :
" Sergeant, throw the picture out, and remove yourself.
Now for some sound legislation. "

Australia and West Australia. Now, how the devil do you make seven out of that?"

TIRED YOUTH: "*I* don't know. One of the clerks made out the beastly list."

HIGH OFFICIAL: "Which clerk?"

TIRED YOUTH: "I don't know. How should I know one beastly clerk from another?"

HIGH OFFICIAL: "Well, you must find out. Seven! There must be two frauds among 'em. Nice we'll look if we let two infernal pickpockets loose among those Indian Rajahs all over diamonds. How are you going to identify 'em when they come? There's one fellow I could swear to, anyhow — a big, hairy, orang-outang of a man about seven feet high. He was here before. I'll swear to *him* anywhere. What was his name again? Gibbs or Gibson, or something like that."

TIRED YOUTH: "Dibbs, I think. Always reminded me of money, I know."

HIGH OFFICIAL: "Well, perhaps it was, but I *think* it was Gibbs. Anyhow, is *he* coming?"

TIRED YOUTH: "I don't know. How should I know? I suppose he is."

HIGH OFFICIAL (at his wits' end): "Well, for goodness sake send someone here that does know. You'll get me into nice trouble, going on like this. Send for a clerk that knows about it, and, meanwhile, we'll have a go at this list of precedence."
(*Tired youth rings bell for clerk, and returns to table to look over list of precedence.*)

HIGH OFFICIAL: "See here, the truth's this. We've got orders from headquarters to soap these confounded self-governing colonies all we can. But, if we send their Premiers in to a function before the Indian Princes — my goodness, the Indians will stick 'em in the back with a *tulwar*, or something. Then there's the Indian, China, Straits Settlement, African, and Crown colonies' lot. Which is to come first, and which last? Have you any idea?"

TIRED YOUTH: "*I* don't know. There's a clerk knows all these things."
(*Enter clerk.*)

HIGH OFFICIAL: "Look here, is there any table of precedence in the office?"

CLERK: "Yes, my Lord."

HIGH OFFICIAL: "Thank God! Who made it out?"

CLERK: "Lord Titmarsh, when he was in office, my Lord."

HIGH OFFICIAL: "Bless him and praise him! See that it is followed with literal accuracy; literal accuracy, you understand — and I'll take all the credit if it goes right, and Titmarsh can take all the blame if it goes wrong. So far, so good. Now there's another thing. How many Premiers are coming from Australia?"

CLERK: "Seven, my Lord!"

HIGH OFFICIAL (*to Tired Youth*): "See! He's made the same mistake you did. If I wasn't here to look after you fellows you'd run the empire to the devil. Seven, indeed!" (To Clerk): "Do you know, sir, there are only five colonies in Australia? Look at the map."

CLERK: "Yes, my Lord; but there's a Premier of Tasmania and a Premier of New Zealand."

HIGH OFFICIAL: "Oh, good gracious! They say America is mostly colonels; this place appears to be mostly Premiers. Now, what do you know about 'em? How are you going to be sure that some fraud doesn't pass himself off as a Premier — some anarchist, with a bomb in his trousers pocket, and blow us all kite-high?"

CLERK: "We have photographs of them all, sir, and a private and confidential cipher report from the Governor of each colony as to their political leanings."

HIGH OFFICIAL: "Let's have a look. Who's this fat, bald-headed man, that looks like a tallow-merchant?"

CLERK: "The Hon. G. H. Reid, my Lord, Premier of New South Wales."

HIGH OFFICIAL (*angrily*): "There you go again! I tell you a man named Gibbs is Premier of New South Wales — great, long, hairy man, quite different from this fellow. I met Gibbs often. This is a fraud, I'll take my oath. Don't he look it — look at his face, all jowl and jelly."

CLERK: "There has been a change of Ministry, my Lord, and this is the present Premier."

HIGH OFFICIAL: "Well, he's not much to look at, anyhow. What does his Governor say about him? Who *is* his Governor, anyhow? Hampden — Oh, I was in the House with Hampden. Dry sort of fellow, not such a fool as he looked. What does he say about him? Let's have a look. (*Reads report mumblingly.*) Truckles to Labor Party ... time server ... not last long ... change may be for the worse ... no force of character ... afraid of the Labor Party ... dare not take K.C.M.G. ... better be bought with a P.C.-ship. I like that — a P.C.-ship indeed for a ruffian like this — an anarchist without the courage of his villainy. We bought Gibbs with a K.C.M.G. Let this ruffian have a K.C.M.G. or nothing."

TIRED YOUTH (*waking to interest in proceedings*): "I read those reports. There's one chappie there rather a good sort. All the rest are awful rotters. Read his report. Nelson I think was the name." (*High Official mumbles over Nelson's report.*) "Fights Labor Party...fearless...can't last long...has worked well for Imperialistic ideas...very courageous man...will support Anglo-Japanese treaty. Ah! that's the sort of man. What's *he* to get?"

TIRED YOUTH: "Headquarters say they are *all* to get P.C.-ships."

HIGH OFFICIAL: "All! Good heavens. Well, if we can't degrade that man Reid in any way, see that he gets the suite of rooms in the worst part of the hotel, and give him a hard seat at all functions. And, by the by, what about taking them round? Who's to do it? *You'll* have to do it: I've got the Canadian and Indian lot to look after."

TIRED YOUTH: "Oh, I'll send one of the clerks and get them tickets for everything that is going in the way of concerts and public receptions and so on. I suppose they can't go to anything really select."

HIGH OFFICIAL (*very slowly and deliberately*): "I should think not. Take 'em to the British Museum and the waxworks, and see that the name of some unattached lord or other is always associated with theirs. It will be put in their cables, and help to damn Reid in the eyes of his friends — and that's about all, isn't it?"

TIRED YOUTH: "And supposing they kick up a row, don't you know, if they're not asked to any of the really swaggah things?"

HIGH OFFICIAL: "My dear boy, if they try anything of that sort on, have them bayoneted by the soldiers the moment they show their noses at the gate. Fill up these P.C. forms, and see that you don't fill 'em up wrong. And now I'm off to the Club. Just be decently civil to these people, but don't go too far, because, you know, by this time next year they will probably be back in their shops selling sugar — I'm certain that man Reid sells sugar, by the look of him. *Au revoir!*"

*Cable item*: All preparations have been made for the reception of the Australian Premiers in London, and they will be the principal items of the Jubilee.

# The Election Season:
## An Illustrated Guide
## for Candidates

### By A. Woodby, M.P.

I HAVE not been asked to contest any electorate, so far, and the letters M.P. after my name do not signify Member of Parliament, but simply Member of the Public. I hold that every white citizen has a right to put what letters he chooses after his name, and I choose to describe myself as M.P.

When I say I have not been asked to contest any electorate, I am not speaking quite accurately. As a matter of fact, a few friends offered to "run me" for the electorate in which I reside. We held a lot of meetings in the back rooms of public houses, and an enormous lot of liquor was consumed at my expense. Every man that heard of it "dropped in", and assured me that my chances were of the brightest. Then each drank about three beers and "dropped out" to pass the word along to his mates, that a candidate was standing drinks, and later on, all the mates dropped in. My meetings were always unanimous in my favour, and I believe I would have beaten George Reid for East Sydney, I was so popular. I employed a man to go round and get signatures to a petition to me to come forward. To make sure that he would work hard, I paid him at so much per hundred signatures. He brought me in a most gratifying list, but I found that most of the signatures were written by the canvasser himself. He took a bottle of ink, a pen, and a rug out to the bush at Bondi, and lay in the sun all day, writing signatures. I found that my friends had "run me" to the tune of twenty pounds, or so, and I stopped my candidature right there. I am prepared, however, to contest any safe seat on either the free trade or protectionist side. And while I am awaiting a requisition, I have decided to make a few notes on canvassing the female vote, which may serve as a guide to my fellow-candidates.

### THE NEED FOR FAT

Every candidate should be a fat man. Not that a fat man is any cleverer than a thin man; but because a superstitious reverence is paid to obesity. A young Boer, writing a book on the war, said that the greatest mistake made by his brave but misguided nation was the reverence paid by them to the old Boers, who were only distinguished by profusion of waistcoat and growth of beard. In fact, he said, worship of hair and tallow had been the ruin of the nation. It is much the same in Australia. Even the gifted Shakespeare, or the person, whoever he was, that wrote his works, says —

> Let me have men about me that are fat;
> Sleek-headed men, and such as sleep o' nights;
> I like not yon lean candidate.

or words to that effect. We may take it, then, that a fat candidate has a tremendous advantage over a thin one.

## FEMALE VOTERS

The female vote is the one that will take some catching at the next election. Unless the women "take to" a man, there is not the least hope of their voting for him, as they are notoriously swayed by their likes and dislikes. The candidate will, therefore, have to be prepared to adapt himself to the various classes he will have to meet: And it is in this adaptability that his chances of success will be.

## THE BARMAID VOTE

To secure this vote you should get yourself up as much like a commercial traveller in jewellery as you can. You should have on a diamond ring that makes the South Head light look like a farthing candle, and a waistcoat that out-Herods Herod in its killing capacities. Conversation should be directed mainly to supper parties after the theatre, and you should smoke a cigar all through the interview, even though it makes you sick afterwards. These things must be gone through if you mean to be a member of Parliament.

## THE SERVANT GIRL VOTE

For the servant girl vote, a disguise in the costume of a policeman is advisable. The candidate may explain in a whisper that he isn't a real policeman, and may work up quite a "penny dreadful" romance out of the situation. If the girl once firmly believes that you are somebody in disguise, her impulsive sympathies will carry her to any lengths. She will poison the family rather than allow them to vote against you. If you don't diguise yourself, the head of the house may never let you see the domestics at all, so the policeman dodge is the best. No one dares to stop a policeman.

## THE LADY POLITICIAN

Having canvassed the barmaids, and the servant girls, you may as well have a trial of strength with the lady politician. Your best attitude is that of abject humility, and the less you say the better. When she asks you, "What do you think of Smith's *Wealth of Nations?*" you must not let her guess that you think she is referring to Bruce Smith. No; rather should you stand in an appealing attitude, and she will proceed to "deal it out of you" by the yard — all you have to do is to listen. No lady politician can keep silent long enough to allow you to answer a question; so, unless you interrupt her, you are safe. Therefore, don't interrupt her. She probably will not think much of you, but she must vote for somebody, and you are as likely as not to be the one.

## THE POTTS POINT VOTE

In canvassing for the female Potts Point vote the candidate should wear a frock coat, eyeglass, spats, and striped trousers. In this class of canvassing it is advisable to adopt what the doctors call a good bedside manner. You should strive to impress the lady with the idea that you are somebody in particular. In these high society circles the great thing is to get the first blow in. On being shown into the room, you should at once say, "Ah, aren't you some relation to my friend Lord Fantod?" If she says, "No, I don't think so," you should say at once, "Ah, pardon me; but I'm sure I heard him mention your name!" That will settle it. You needn't say anything more. That woman will tell her husband she is going to vote for you whether he likes it or not, and if he says, "Why?" she will say, "Because he knows Lord Fantod." That will dispose of one class of female voter.

## THE ROCKS PUSH

Last, but not least, comes the Rocks lady. To canvass this class is a matter of risk. To begin with, your wife may stop you if she gets any idea where you are off to. Then, if you can dodge her, the risks are great of being "topped off with a bottle", or disposed of by the admirers of the lady you approach. A good suit of clothing provokes open hostility. The candidate's only chance is to get a pair of bell-bottoms, high-heeled boots, and a soft hat. Just walk past the lady a few times, and look hard at her, and she will say, "Hullo, Face," and the rest is easy. The "lidy", if she likes the look of you, will vote for you, and if she doesn't she won't. And that is all there is to say about it.

In canvassing about the Rocks, you must always be ag'in the Government. Talk in a dark way about "blokes that puts themselves into good billets", and be severe on everybody, and you can't go wrong.

Now and again, you will meet a lady voter who has made a study of politics, and has read all the democratic papers. If this disastrous fate befalls you, the only thing to do is "bluff". On no account must you betray any hesitation — if you do you are lost. If fairly cornered, you can always fall back on Coghlan. Coghlan has helped many a lame political dog over a stile. If you are challenged as to any facts, you should begin the debate by asking, "Have you seen the last volume of Coghlan?" Of course she hasn't. Then you can say with a mysterious air, "Well, look at Coghlan, an' you'll see all that clearly laid out." Then leave before you get laid out yourself. If you have a good florid bluff manner, you will hear the push say as you leave, "An' 'e's a scholar, that bloke. Knows Coghlan like a book." For foreign facts, always refer to Mulhall. If they ask, "Who is Mulhall?" say he wrote the political columns in *Reynolds Weekly* for years. They won't know any better. But whatever you do, in dealing with the Rocks vote, never get confused or "lose your block", as the saying is. You may be "topped off" at any minute if you do.

These few hints are put forward in the hope that they may save the breath of many worthy persons, who would otherwise waste a lot of energy in what is called "hot air talk" to female voters. Politics don't matter: clothes are the main thing.

# THE COMIC AUSTRALIAN

Registered at the G.P.O. for transmission by Post as a Newspaper.

## A JOURNAL OF FACT, FUN, AND FICTION.

Vol. 2, No. 36.          JUNE 4, 1912.          Price, One Penny.

O'Malley: "See, there's your Capitol, Jim."

M'Gowen (still near-sighted): "Yes, but where's the capital for the Capitol?"

O' Malley: " See, there's your Capitol, Jim. "

M' Gowen ( still near-sighted ) : " Yes, but where's the capital for the Capitol? "

# The Oracle on the Capital Site

"MY GRANDDAUGHTER," said the Oracle, when he met the Thin Man on Monday morning on the Block in George Street, "my granddaughter, who was married about a year ago, was kind enough to present me with a great-grandson yesterday."

"Good gracious!" said the Thin Man.

"Yes, it makes a person feel a trifle patriarchal," admitted the Oracle, "but the young mother is but little more than forty years my junior. She is my daughter's daughter. I have suggested that the little boy who made his debut yesterday shall be named Methuselah."

"After yourself?"

"Certainly not. Old I may be, but not so old as all that. The original Methuselah, although not a Government pensioner, lived to be 969 years old, and if he were possessed of any considerable property his heirs and assigns must have grown extremely tired waiting for the old gentleman to 'throw the seven', if I may be allowed a somewhat flippant expression. Among patriarchs in days of old, of course, 400 or 500 years was not regarded as unseemly delay in giving somebody else a chance, but the effort of Methuselah to last for ten centuries — in which he very nearly succeeded — could not be considered a fair thing by those naturally entitled to the reversion of the old gentleman's real and personal estate. I wish my great-grandson to be called Methuselah, in the hope that he may live as long as his historic namesake, for I feel a desire, my friend — a strange yearning, as it were — to gaze upon the face of some human creature who may live to see the Federal capital established in New South Wales, as provided in the Constitution Act. Should the little Methuselah who appeared for the first time yesterday live for ten centuries or thereabouts it is possible that he may see the terms of the compact carried out. Such a sight is not for our eyes, my friend, nor for the eyes of our children or grand-children; but I have a lingering hope — something tells me — that should my little great-grandson live for ten centuries he will see the Federal Capital established, unless Australia is annexed by the Japanese in the meantime."

"Oh, we'll have the capital long before that!" said the Thin Man, hopefully.

"You think so," said the Oracle, "and so do other people, but I don't. I am not one of those who believe in underestimating the astuteness of a rival. The politicians of Victoria are more astute than ours. The boycotting of Sydney as a capital was a stroke of genius — positive genius! If Sydney could be selected, New South Wales would be practically unanimous as to where the capital should be. Inside the proscribed area more than half the people live; outside the proscribed area there are 495 districts, all struggling against each other to be selected."

"Nonsense," said the Thin Man.

"Nonsense?" repeated the Oracle. "You mustn't suppose that, because only half a dozen possible sites are mentioned, there are no others. There are dozens and scores of other possible sites — any site is possible, so long as it isn't within a hundred miles of where it ought to be. But they don't want to trot them all out at once — half a dozen rival sites at a time is quite enough to prevent anything definite being done; and then, if any agreement should be come to about them, they have official inspections and picnics for another half dozen. The Constitution doesn't bar Albury or Broken Hill, Bourke or Tenterfield. There are quite 495 places that have a chance of being selected; in fact, any place that is not within 100 miles of Sydney may have a chance."

"Buckley's chance," said the Thin Man.

"Just so," said the Oracle, "but legally they all have a chance. If the representatives of N.S.W. would work together to see the bargain adhered to, the matter might be settled in a couple of centuries, or even earlier; but everything is in favour of delay, not merely temporary delay, but eternal, everlasting delay. What are all these fresh picnic excursions for?"

"I suppose they like picnics," said the Thin Man.

"Of course they do," said the Oracle; "but if they ever do select a site in N.S.W. there will be no further excuse for picnics. Talk and tucker is one main factor of delay, feeding and orating!"

"Is that why they call it Feed-oration?" asked the Thin Man.

"That's one reason," said the Oracle. "The picnic obstacle is being worked for all it is worth. Because there are some new members in the Federal Parliament, they all have to be taken on picnic excursions to the possible sites. Was there ever a Parliament dissolved of which all the members were re-elected? Never in the history of the British Empire. There are always new members in every new Parliament, and if the picnic inspection is to be renewed for the guidance of new members after every general election, that alone will be quite sufficient to delay the matter for ever. But that's not the only factor."

"No?"

"No, indeed," said the Oracle. "Suppose the Federal Parliament determined to select a site at once, and did so?"

"That would settle the matter," said the Thin Man.

"Oh, would it?" said the Oracle. "In the first place, Mr Chapman wants the capital in his electorate, and Sir William Lyne is the same, and so are all the other members in regard to their electorates, or nearly all of them. It is almost impossible for them to agree upon a site. Mr Chapman hasn't made up his mind yet as to which part of his electorate he would prefer to see selected as the capital; neither has Sir William Lyne. And they are the N.S.W. members of the Federal Cabinet! But supposing all these rivalries were got over and the Government determined on one site, and Mr Watson were given a portfolio to induce the Labour Party to support, and the Opposition, for the sake of political honesty, offered to support the selection of any site at all, what then?"

"Surely that would settle the question?" asked the Thin Man.

"No, it wouldn't," said the Oracle, "not by a jugful! I suppose you know that if the capital ever is in New South Wales there will have to be public buildings for Parliament, the Law Courts, the Government departments, and so on."

"Certainly," said the Thin Man.

"Well," said the Oracle, "will all these palatial buildings spring up like mushrooms when Alfred Deakin waves a magician's wand over the selected area? Is Alfred Deakin the modern embodiment of Aladdin of the Wonderful Lamp?"

"Of course he isn't," asserted the Thin Man.

"Well how are these palaces to be built when the State of N.S.W. can't borrow enough money to pay the interest on what it owes already?"

"We wouldn't have to pay all the cost," said the Thin Man.

"The other States would very properly take all sorts of care that we paid our full share of it, if not more. In the Centennial year — sixteen years ago — Lord Carrington laid the foundation stone of new Parliament Houses for New South Wales in the Domain. The foundation stone is still there, unless somebody has run away with it; but where are the new Parliament Houses? Not there, my child! Not there!"

"Don't call me a child," said the Thin Man.

"You are but an infant to me," said the Oracle. "Do you think, if a site were selected, say at Dead Horse Gully; in Sir William Lyne's electorate; or at Cow Flat, among Mr Chapman's constituents, do you think Alfred Deakin would hire a tent from Fitzgerald Brothers' Circus to be the meeting place of the Federal Legislature? Would he ask the Governor-General and suite to camp in a stringybark hut? Would you like to see Sir Samuel Griffith and his brother judges of the High Court sitting on gin cases in the bush to hear an appeal case, from the New South Wales Supreme Court?"

"But," protested the Thin Man, "the politicians ought to settle the capital question."

"Settle it?" repeated the Oracle. "Settle the capital question? They are capable of settling anything, and if they haven't settled Australia altogether it isn't for want of trying! Yes, I hope that great-grandson of mine may live to be as old as the original Methuselah, and then he may see the Federal capital in New South Wales. Let's go in here and drink his health."

And they did.

# A War Office in Trouble

## A Sketch at the Time of the Boer War

SCENE: War Office, London. Telephones are ringing, typewriters clicking, clerks in dozens rushing hither and thither at express rate. An atmosphere of feverish unrest hangs over everything. In the passages and lobbies crowds of military contractors, officials, newspapermen and inventors of patent guns have been waiting for hours to get a few minutes' interview with those in authority. Mounted messengers dash up to the door every few seconds. In the innermost room of all, a much-decorated military veteran with a bald head, a grizzled moustache and an eyeglass is dictating to three shorthand writers at once, while clerks rush in and out with cablegrams, letters and cards from people waiting. On the table are littered a heap of lists of troops, army-contracts, and tenders for supplies, all marked "Urgent". A clerk rushes in.

CLERK: "Cablegram from Australia offering troops, sir!"

MILITARY VETERAN: "No! Can't have 'em. It has been decided not to use blacks, except as a last resource."

CLERK: "But these are white troops, sir — the local forces. It is officially desired that they be taken if possible."

MILITARY VETERAN: "Who is the Australian Commander-in-Chief? I didn't know they had an army at all. I knew they had police, of course!"

CLERK: "There are seven distinct cablegrams, sir; seven distinct Commanders-in-Chief all offering troops."

M.V. (*roused to excitement*): "Great Heavens! are they going to take the war off our hands? *Seven* Commanders-in-Chief! They must have been quietly breeding armies all these years in Australia. Let's have a look at the cables. Where's this from?"

C: "Tasmania, sir. They offer to send a Commander-in-Chief and" (pauses, aghast) "and *eighty-five* men!"

M.V. (*jumping to his feet*): "What! Have I wasted all this time talking about eighty-five men! You must be making a mistake!"

C: "No, sir. It says eighty-five men!"

M.V.: "Well I *am* damned! Eighty-five men! You cable back and say that I've seen bigger armies on the stage at Drury Lane Theatre. Just wire and say *this* isn't a pantomime. They haven't got to march round and round a piece of scenery. Tell 'em to stop at home and *breed!*" (*Resumes dictation*.) "At least five thousand extra men should be sent from India in addition to —"

C: "Cabinet instructions are to take these troops, whether they're any good or not, sir. Political reasons!"

M.V. (*with a sigh*): "Well, let 'em come. Let 'em *all* come — the whole eighty-five! But don't let it leak out, or the Boers will say we're not playing 'em fair. Tell 'em to send infantry, anyhow; we don't want horses eating their heads off."

C. (*interrupts again*): "These other colonies, sir — are we to accept 'em all?"

M.V.: "Yes. Didn't I say let 'em *all* come? There'll be plenty of room for 'em in South Africa. They won't feel crowded." (*Resumes dictation*.) "The expenditure of a hundred thousand pounds at least will be needed to —"

C: "They want to know, if they pay the men's fares over, will the British Government pay their return fares?"

M.V.: "Yes, I should think we would. We'll put 'em in the front and there won't be so many of 'em left to go back. If the colonies had any sense *they'd* have paid the return fares. Now, please go away and let me get to work."

(*Ten minutes later, clerk timidly reappears.*)
C: "If you please, sir, another cable from New South Wales. They say they would sooner send artillery!"

M.V.: "Oh, blast it all! What does their artillery amount to?"

C: "One battery, sir".

M.V.: "*One* battery! Well, they've got to come, I suppose. 'Cry havoc and let slip the dogs of war.' Stop their one battery if you can; but if not, let it come. And now go, and don't let me have any more of you." (*Resumes dictation, and has just got to "the purchase of ten thousand horses" when the Clerk reappears.*)

C: "Fresh cable, sir! Two circus proprietors in Sydney have presented six circus horses —"

M.V.: "Shivering Sheol! This is the climax! Six circus horses! Didn't they say anything about a clown and pantaloon? Surely they wouldn't see the Empire hurled to ruin for want of a clown. Perhaps they could let us have a few sword-swallowers to get off with the Boers' weapons? Look here, now — hand the whole thing over to one of the senior clerks, and tell him to do exactly what he d —— well pleases in the matter, but that if he comes in here to ask any questions about it, I'll have him shot! Now go, and don't you come here any more, or I'll have *you* shot too. Take this cheque for a hundred thousand to the petty cash department, and tell that contractor outside that his tender is two millions over the estimate, and don't let me hear any more of this blessed Australian army."

*Cable message*: Some difficulty exists in ascertaining from the War Office whether the colonial troops will be expected to take their own saddles or not, and whether the officer commanding shall take one horse or two. It is not definitely known whether the offer of Fitzgeralds' six circus horses will be accepted. Great enthusiasm prevails.

Australia's offer to send troops to serve with the English forces in South Africa resulted in the contribution of 848 officers, 15,327 other ranks and 16,314 horses.

# A General Inspection

## FROM *ARMY SKETCHES*

"WHEN'S THE General's inspection?" inquired the cook, uneasily, of the Orderly Room Sergeant. The Sergeant, being Scotch, and in daily converse with "The Heads", was always supposed to know everything about everybody in the military world.

"What are you worrying about?" he said.

"You never know what a General'll want", the cook explained. "One's all for drill, another for shootin'; and all that. One come one day, and it seems his dream was to have every officer know the men's names and all about 'em. Our captain had been put fly to this, so he sez to us, just before the General came round, 'Whatever name I give you men today, see you answer to it', he says. So the General come along the line, lookin' at our boots and feelin' our toonics between his finger and thumb, because some of 'em were different issue to the others; and all of a sudden he points to me, and he sez, "What's that man's name?", he sez. An', of course, our Captain knew my name all right; but bein' ast sudden that way, he got rattled and outs with the first name he can think of. 'His name's McFarland,' he says. Well, there was a McFarland about ten paces further down the line; and just as the General comes opposite to him, he halts and snaps out, 'Trooper McFarland, two paces to the front, march!' He wanted to see if our Captain had give me the right name or not. So o' course, this real McFarland, he steps out, and I steps out, too. And the General lamps us a bit, and he says, 'What's this?' he says. 'Is there two McFarlands, are you brothers?' he says. So I says 'Yes, sir', and the other real McFarland he says, 'No, sir', both together, just like that: and, of course, the General went off a treat. So you see, Scotty, you want to know what this one will ask?"

The Orderly Sergeant was quite in the dark as to what form the General's questions were likely to take, so he side-stepped the problem.

"Nobody keers whit happens tae a kuk," he said.

"Oh! don't they!" said the cook. "That's all you know. I bet you the General'll ask me more questions than any man in the Regiment."

All this Scotty pondered till you could almost hear his brain working; and then he put forward a valuable suggestion.

EASTER MANOEUVRES.

" To-day's work of the infantry brigades at camp was of the nature
of what is known in schools of instruction as a ' refresher' course. " – News Item

"He'll go tae the Light Horrse lines before he comes here", he said. "You step over to yon Light Horrse kuk-house, and find out what he asks them, an' ye'll be a' richt!"

It was a quarter of a mile to the Light Horse cook-house; and a half mile walk on a hot day over loose desert sand did not appeal to our cook, who is a credit to his own cooking: but he saw nothing else for it, so he set off doggedly to plod over the sand in the blazing heat and disappeared among the Light Horse tents. Soon we saw the cavalcade of the inspecting General moving slowly up the Light Horse lines, and with our mental vision, we could see, and with the ear of imagination we could hear, the General pointing with his cane and asking why the tent flaps were not rolled evenly, and why there were so many Egyptian beds in the tents.

There came a long halt before the Light Horse cook-house: and it is a singular fact the Generals often show great interest in the doings of cooks. One has been known, after shaking everybody from the C.O. to the Company Sergeant Major to their foundations, to speak quite pleasantly with the cooks, and ask them what they did for a living before the war. Possibly the reason for this is, that an army travels on its stomach, and the cook is really a very important man. "No cook, no company" would be a very good military maxim to be elaborated in lectures at Duntroon and elsewhere.

At last the General moved away from the Light Horse cook-house, and soon afterwards we could see our own cook in the distance ploughing his way back through the sand. When he arrived he was sweating profusely, but wore a contented look. The Orderly Room Sergeant had made a job for himself to take some papers to the Quartermaster's, so as to escape for a while from the state of high nervous tension that prevails in an orderly room when a general inspection is on. He hailed the cook as he passed.

"Find oot onything?" he said.

"I think so", said the cook. "I went to both cook-houses after the Head had been there; and he ast each of 'em whether they gave the men roast meat or only stoos. He roared one of 'em up a treat for not having an oven to roast meat in. Roast meat!"

By this time the General rode up, with his A.D.C., and the local Commandant the regulation distance behind him. He noted whether the Officers' Mess room was in good order, and whether the mess orderly was tidy. For it is by details that military shows are judged: and incident to this it may be mentioned that one of the greatest station inspectors in Australia once said that he always judged a station manager by his gates. If the gates were in good order, then everything else was likely to be in good order: by their gates ye shall know them! But to return to the inspection.

The General, having immediately awarded full points for neatness of turn-out to the officers' mess, and for speed, style and action to the mess orderly, set off round the camp. At the first squadron, the squadron leader rode up and saluted and fell in beside the General to receive whatever of praise or blame might be coming his way. Now, the squadron leader had put in a couple of anxious hours going about his lines, seeing that the white stones round the camp were nicely whitewashed, all dunnage and litter out of the road, everybody dressed correctly, and so on. But he had made his inspection on foot, and, not being able to see to the roofs of the sheds, had missed the fact that all the natives employed in the lines had stacked their *gallabiehs* on the roof of one of the sheds. The General's eagle eye fell on this: "What have you got up on that roof", he said, "an old clothes store?" Then he found a fire bucket empty and volunteered the remark, that fire buckets without water in them would not be of much use in case of a conflagration. "You can't put out fires with 'eye-wash', you know", he said, pointing to the rows of beautifully whitewashed stones on which such hopes had been built. In fact, things were going badly all along the line, and it was felt that it rested with the cook-house to redeem the day. Had not all the cook-house staff once been awarded a prize of two pounds for the best and cleanest cook-house in camp? All was not yet lost!

The General rode up to the cook-house and the cook came out, saluted, and stood to attention. The General asked the usual questions as to how long the cook had been at the job and whether he was a cook in civil life, to which latter question he received the reply that the cook, in private life, was a revolving window shutter manufacturer! Not being able to carry the conversation further in that line, the General turned to the cook-house.

"Very good", he said. "No flies. Sink in good order. Brick floor. Very clean. What did the men have for breakfast this morning?"

"Porridge and bacon, Sir; and most of 'em buys a few eggs, and I fry 'em."

"Very good. And what did they have for dinner?"

Now the men had had stew for dinner, but the cook wasn't going to say so. He had not walked half a mile in the heat and sand for nothing.

"They had roast meat and baked potatoes and puddin'," he said.

"Very good. That's it. Not too much stew. Feed men well, and they'll do well at any job. Very satisfactory."

The day was saved. Our cook had redeemed the honour of the Regiment; but alas, just as the General drew his bridle to move off, his eye lit on the cook's bare, hairy chest, which was exposed by an open shirt.

"Where's your identity disc?" said the General.

**DOWNRIGHT CRUELTY**

"Look 'ere, I reckon it's a blanky shame to force my poor boy to go to compulsory trainin'
on a blazin' 'ot day like this. I was goin' ter let 'im chop wood for a few hours."

A personal search revealed, that not only the cook, but two of his assistants were minus their discs. The General moved on without a word. And thus it was that our report of the inspection contained the dreadful sentence: "A little more attention to details would be desirable". And thus it was that our cook trod the orderly room tarpaulin next morning on a charge of "neglect, to the prejudice of good order and military discipline in that he omitted to wear his identity disc".

"There you are", said the cook, "me walkin' all that way to the Light Horse for nothin'. I wish I'd told him the men had stoo for dinner. He'd a gone that wild, he wouldn't ha' noticed the identity disc!"

# A Yellow Gloom

## An Informal Letter from London

I ARRIVED in London on the evening of the record fog; the whole city was choking in a kind of yellow gloom, out of which the whistles of the bus conductors and shouts of cabmen rose like the din of fiends in a pit of torment. The theatres nearly all closed their doors. Trafalgar Square was full of buses all night; buses that had failed to make their way home, and simply pulled up and waited for daylight, with their passengers huddled inside; the cabmen wouldn't even try to take people home — a five-pound note was vainly offered by one man for a drive of half an hour — what would have been half an hour's drive if there had been any light, or even any decent sort of darkness to drive by; but this awful yellow shroud choked everything; and yet, talking it over with an English bus driver next morning he said with the greatest pride, "Ah! You don't see fogs like that in no other part of the world!" There is a beautiful serene self-complacency about these people that one can never sufficiently admire. We were moving up the Strand in a stream of traffic, doing about four miles an hour, halted every now and again by policemen, the old well-trained bus horses picking their way along like two well-regulated machines; and the busman said to me with conscious superiority, "Ah! You don't see drivin' like this in no other part of the world!" I thought of various little bits of driving that I had seen some of Cobb and Co.'s men do on dark nights with unbroken horses in very broken country; but I didn't try to tell the busman about them.

> What do they understand?
> Beefy face and grubby 'and.

He went on placidly, "Ah, London for me; all the luxuries of the world come to London; the best of everythink's good enough for us; and it's a healthy place too. Look at me. I'm past fifty, and I'm sixteen hours a day on this bus."

I thought he must have a lot of time to enjoy luxuries.

# The Oracle on Music and Singing

"HELLO!" SAID the Oracle, as he met the Thin Man on George Street, "fancy me eating you! as the cat said to the mouse. Quite a treat to get a dry afternoon in this drought-stricken country, isn't it?"

"We've certainly had a lot of rain here," replied the Thin Man; "but I hear it is very dry in the interior."

"So it is," said the Oracle, "so it is. Let us, therefore, proceed to irrigate the interior before we go any further."

And they entered a corner hostelry, whence they presently emerged, the Thin Man wiping his mouth.

"If you must wipe your mouth after imbibing," said the Oracle; "you should do so before leaving the hotel. It does not look well as you are stepping out into the street."

"Oh, there is no pretence about me," replied the Thin Man, in a boastful tone. "I am no humbug."

"Just so," said the Oracle, "that is your way of putting it. Another, and perhaps, a more correct way, would be to say that you are lost to all sense of shame."

"Sir!" exclaimed the indignant Thin Man.

"Don't get your hair off," said the Oracle; "you wouldn't look half as pretty with a bald head."

The twain had walked along until they came abreast of a large music warehouse, standing in front of which was a short, stout gentleman with long hair, a Kaiser Wilhelm moustache, a pair of pince-nez, and a broad-brimmed sombrero jauntily poised on one side of his head.

"Ah!" said the Oracle, "there is my friend, Herr Walzer Wiegenlied. I have heard — but, of course, you needn't mention it — that his real name is James Smith. Of course, he had to adopt another; no man could possibly hope to succeed as a music teacher if he bore the name of James Smith. He must also let his hair grow long. Some of them do that for appearance sake, and others, perhaps, because they lack the necessary sixpence demanded by the relentless tonsorial artist."

"Sir Arthur Sullivan," said the Thin Man, "did not use to get himself up like Buffalo Bill or a Spanish brigand, did he?"

"Well no," said the Oracle. "On the contrary, Sir Arthur wore a moustache of modest size, mutton-chop whiskers, and short-cropped hair. He also dressed like an ordinary person, and looked more like a stockbroker or an attorney than a musician. But Sullivan was immensely successful with his beautiful melodies; and could, therefore, afford to despise the idea that eccentricity is genius! But Walzer Wiegenlied is a very good fellow, indeed. He has often told me that the broad hat and long hair idea is absurd; but, at the same time, he feels compelled to follow the fashion of the musical world, lest it should be thought that by getting his hair cut short, and wearing a hard felt hat, he was trying to show off. It is not a matter of personal taste; it is a question of professional necessity. The public would never believe a man was a first-class violinist if he had his hair cropped short, and called himself Jim Smith. So our friend has long hair and calls himself Herr Walzer Wiegenlied — *Walzer*, of course, is waltz, and *Wiegenlied* means a lullaby — 'Mummer's Little Alabama Coon', as it were. But he knows me well, and he'll wonder what we've stuck here so long for, jabbering away. Come along and I'll introduce you. Good fellow, Jim is; always willing to do the amiable with a couple of friends when he has ninepence."

"*Ah, mein Herr! Gut morgen!*" said the Oracle to Professor Wiegenlied.

"Morgan was a bushranger," muttered the Thin Man to himself, "this cove looks more like a circus cowboy."

"The others did not hear this *sotto voce* criticism, and the Professor and the Thin Man were duly introduced.

"I am always pleased to meet a musician," said the Thin Man, as he shook hands with Professor Wiegenlied. "Music", as Shakespeare says, 'hath charms to soothe the savage beast'."

"Breast," corrected the Oracle; "savage breast, not savage beast."

"Oh," said the Thin Man, "I always thought it was savage beast, in fact, I thought that explained why people generally put a brass band round a bulldog's neck!"

"Well, gentlemen," said the Professor, "my class is over for this morning, and I was about to drink success to a new venture I have in hand. Will you join me? I am neither as rich as Rockefeller, nor as poor as Job; but fortunately I had a pupil taken away by an indignant parent this morning."

"Do you call that fortunate?" was the Oracle's dubious query.

"Certainly," said the Professor, "very fortunate. I had to teach the young lady to sing and to play also, and she could do neither, and never will. She has no ear at all. It would make your blood run cold to listen to her. But her parents thought she could be taught. It is impossible; she doesn't know a bar of music from a bar of soap, and she never will. I am very glad she is gone."

"But you lose a pupil," said the Oracle.

"I lose a pupil, but I get my pay," said the Professor. "There are some parents who while their children are doing well never think of paying, but let the fees run on. But, of course, when they grow indignant because you haven't made another Melba of their own little Mary Ann, and resolve to take the pupil away, they must pay up, if only to preserve their own dignity. Let us come in here and have a chat until lunch time," he added, pushing open the side door, and entering the saloon bar.

The three sat around a marble table, and Professor Wiegenlied "did the amiable".

"I am sorry you don't speak German," said the Professor, "as I have to keep in practice. My own compositions are of the Wagnerian because it is the easiest, and suits my professional name best."

"I thought," said the Oracle, "that Wagner's music was very difficult."

"It is very difficult to understand," said the Professor, "and that is why so many people pretend to appreciate it; but, to a musician, the Wagnerian style is like rolling off a log, for though you must write a lot of chords, and break off here and there into a minor key that sounds like a dog moaning with the stomach ache, you need no tune."

"No tune!" exclaimed the Oracle.

"I don't mean that Wagner never composed a melody," said the Professor, "because that would be absurd; but much of his music is so smothered in strange chords that the melody hasn't a possible chance to get into the ear of the auditor; it is crowded out for want of space and Wagner's disciples, of whom I am one, have abandoned the idea of having any tune in the music. Makes composition so much easier; that is why I took up Wagner, and adopted a German name. Don't you know German at all?"

"Only wurst and sauerkraut and pretzel and lager bier," said the Oracle, "and we could hardly keep up a conversation on that."

"And you?" asked the Professor of the Thin Man.

"I know only this," said the Thin Man:

> *Gott erhalte unzern Kaiser!*
> *Unzern gooten Kaiser Bill!*

"I'm afraid we'd better stick to the vernacular tongue of Balmain, Bloomsbury and the Bowery," said the Professor.

"Although I am not a professional musician," said the Oracle to the Thin Man, "I understand a good deal about it and more particularly of the business part of the profession. It is on my advice that our friend proposes to recommend that no fewer than six of his pupils shall be sent to Paris to finish their musical training under Madame Whatsthis."

Proud Parent : " What do you think of her execution? "
Fed-up Friend : " Oh, I'm very much in favour of it. "

"Marchesi," interpolated the Professor.

"Ma Casey!" repeated the Thin Man. "Is she Irish?"

"Of course not! She's French," said the Professor.

"Name sounds Irish," murmured the Thin Man.

"Six entertainments," went on the Oracle, "will be given in the Town Hall, and subscription lists will be opened. Other teachers of music have been content to discover one genius at a time; it is on my advice that our friend has determined to discover half a dozen. The Sydney people are always willing to send some really good singers abroad. If the singers are only middling, or so-so, as Touchstone says, we are loth to part with them; if they are bad we refuse to part with them at any price; but when they are really good we insist upon them going away to the other end of the world, and staying there as long as possible. We do the same with musicians as with singers; we provide them with the means to go away and stay away. The rule in England is just the opposite. When a German band is playing outside a house in the West End of London, the footman or the page boy is sent out to inform the bandmaster that he will get a half-crown to go away at once, a shilling if he gets through in ten minutes, and nothing at all if he stays for a quarter of an hour. They pay bad musicians to go away; we offer inducements to the best musicians to leave; and if a violinist happens to be born in Sydney and hampered with the unclassical name of Brown, his only possible chance of appreciation in his native village is to wear a sombrero like our friend here, let his hair grow long, and call himself Monsieur Le Brun. With a foreign name and a foreign appearance, an Australian musician has a chance in his own country; with his hair cut short and a hard-hitter hat he has no more chance of being fairly appreciated than the late lamented Mr Buckley."

"Fillemupagen," said Professor Wiegenlied to the lady behind the bar.

"Is that German?" asked the Thin Man.

"No" said the Professor, "that's Volapuk, the universal language!"

"Ah," said the Oracle, "they may talk of singers as they please, but I'd sooner have a fiver than a tenor!"

Then they arose and departed their several ways.

# The Amateur Gardener

THE FIRST step in amateur gardening is to sit down and consider what good you are going to get by it. If you are only a tenant by the month, as most people are, it is obviously not much use your planting a fruit orchard or an avenue of oak trees, which will take years to come to maturity. What you want is something that will grow quickly, and will stand transplanting for when you move it would be a sin to leave behind you all the plants on which you have spent so much labour and so much patent manure. We knew a man once who was a bookmaker by trade — and a leger bookmaker at that — but he had a passion for horses and flowers, and when he "had a big win", as he occasionally did, it was his custom to have movable wooden stables built on skids put up in the yard, and to have tons of the best soil that money could buy carted into he garden of the premises which he was occupying. Then he would keep splendid horses in the stables, grow rare roses and show-bench chrysanthemums in the garden and the landlord passing by would see the garden in a blaze of colour, and would promise himself that he would raise the bookmaker's rent next quarter day. However, when the bookmaker "took the knock", as he invariably did at least twice a year, it was his pleasing custom to move without giving any notice. He would hitch two carthorses to the stables, and haul them away at night. He would dig up not only the roses, trees, and chrysanthemums that he had planted, but would also cart away the soil he had brought in; in fact, he used to shift the garden bodily. He had one garden that he shifted to nearly every suburb in Sydney in turn, and he always argued that change of air was invaluable for chrysanthemums. Be this as it may, the proposition is self-evident that the would-be amateur gardener should grow flowers not for his landlord, nor for his creditors, but for himself.

Being determined then to go in for gardening on commonsense principles, and having decided on the class of shrubs that you mean to grow, the next thing is to consider what sort of a chance you have of growing them. If your neighbour keeps game fowls it may be taken for granted that before long they will pay you a visit, and you will see the rooster scratching your pot plants out by the roots as if they were so much straw, just to make a nice place to lie down and fluff the dust over himself. Goats will also stray in from the street, and bite the young shoots off, selecting the most valuable plants with a discrimination that would do credit to a professional gardener; and whatever valuable plant a goat bites is doomed. It is therefore useless thinking of growing any delicate or squeamish plants. Most amateur gardeners maintain a lifelong struggle against the devices of Nature, and when the forces of man and the forces of Nature come into conflict Nature will win every time. Nature has decreed that certain plants shall be hardy, and therefore suitable to suburban amateur gardens, but the suburban amateur gardener persists in trying to grow quite other plants, and in despising those marked out by Nature for his use. It is to correct this tendency that this article is written.

The greatest standby to the amateur gardener should undoubtedly be the blue-flowered shrub known as plumbago. This homely but hardy plant will grow anywhere. It naturally prefers a good soil and a sufficient rainfall, but if need be it will worry along without either. Fowls cannot scratch it up, and even a goat turns away dismayed from its hard-featured branches. The flower is not strikingly beautiful nor ravishingly scented, but it flowers nine months out of the year, and though smothererd with street dust and scorched by the summer sun you will find that faithful old plumbago plugging along undismayed. A plant like this should be encouraged and made much of, but the misguided amateur gardener as a rule despises it. The plant known as the churchyard geranium is also one marked out by Providence for the amateur, as is also cosmea, a plant that comes up year after year when once planted. In creepers, bignonia and lantana will hold their own

KILLED BY KINDNESS
Wife: "Fred, do you suppose that if we took as good a care of the weeds as we do the vegetables it would kill them?"

under difficulties perhaps as well as any that can be found. In trees, the Port Jackson fig is a patriotic plant to grow, and it is a fine plant to provide exercise, as it sheds its leaves unsparingly, and requires to have the whole garden swept up every day. Your aim as a student of Nature should be to encourage the survival of the fittest. In grasses, too, the same principle holds good. There is a grass called nut grass, and another called Parramatta grass, either of which will hold its own against anything living or dead. The average gardening manual gives you recipes for destroying these grasses. Why should you destroy them in favour of a sickly plant that needs constant attention? No. The Parramatta grass is the selected of Nature, and who are you to interfere with Nature?

Having thus decided to go in for strong, simple plants that will hold their own, and a bit over, you must get your implements of husbandry. A spade is the first thing, but the average ironmonger will show you an unwieldy weapon only meant to be used by navvies. Don't buy it. Get a small spade, about half-size — it is nice and light and doesn't tire the wrist, and with it you can make a good display of enthusiasm, and earn the hypocritical admiration of your wife. After digging for half an hour or so, you can get her to rub your back with any of the backache cures advertised in this journal and from that moment you will have no further need for the spade.

Besides a spade, a barrow is about the only other thing needed, and anyhow it is almost a necessity for removing cases of whisky into the house. A rake is useful sometimes as a weapon, when your terrier dog has bailed up a cat, and will not attack it till the cat is made to run. And talking of terrier dogs, an acquaintance of ours has a dog that does all his gardening. The dog is a small elderly terrier, whose memory is failing somewhat, so as soon as the terrier has planted a bone in the garden the owner slips over and digs it up and takes it away. When the terrier goes back and finds the bone gone, he distrusts his own memory, and begins to think that perhaps he has made a mistake, and has dug in the wrong place; so he sets to work and digs patiently all over the garden, turning over acres of soil in his search for the missing bone. Meanwhile, the man saves himself a lot of backache.

The sensible amateur gardener, then, will not attempt to fight with Nature but will fall in with her views. What more pleasant than to get out of bed at 11.30 on a Sunday morning, and look out of your window at a lawn waving with the feathery plumes of Parramatta grass, and to see beyond it the churchyard or stinking geranium flourishing side by side with the plumbago and the Port Jackson fig? The garden gate blows open, and the local commando of goats, headed by an aged and fragrant patriarch (locally known as De Wet from the impossibility of capturing him), rush in; but their teeth will barely bite through the wiry stalks of the Parramatta grass, and the plumbago and the fig tree fail to attract them; and before long they scale the fence by standing on one another's shoulders, and disappear into the next-door garden, where a fanatic is trying to grow show roses. After the last goat has scaled your neighbour's fence, and only De Wet is left in your garden, your little dog discovers him, and De Wet beats a hurried retreat, apparently at full speed, with the little dog exactly one foot behind him in frantic pursuit. We say apparently at full speed, because old experience has taught that De Wet can run as fast as a greyhound when he likes; but he never exerts himself to go any faster than is necessary to just keep in front of whatever dog is after him; in fact, De Wet once did run for about a hundred yards with a greyhound after him, and then he suddenly turned and butted the greyhound cranksided, as Uncle Remus would say. Hearing the scrimmage, your neighbour comes onto his verandah, and sees the chase going down the street. "Ha! that wretched old De Wet again!" he says. "Small hope your dog has of catching him! Why don't you get a garden gate like mine, so as he won't get in?" "No; he can't get in at your gate," is the reply, "but I think his commando are in your back garden now." The next thing is a frantic rush by your neighbour, falling downstairs in his haste, and the sudden reappearance of the commando skipping easily back over the fence, and through your gate into the street again, stopping to bite some priceless pot plants of your neighbour's as they come out. A horse gets in, but his hoofs make no impression on the firm turf of the Parramatta grass, and you get quite a hearty laugh by dropping a chair on him out of the first floor window, and seeing him go tearing down the street. The game fowls of your other neighbour come fluttering into your garden, and scratch and chuckle and fluff themselves under your plumbago bush; but you don't worry. Why should you? They can't hurt it: and besides, you know well enough that the small black hen and the big yellow hen, who have disappeared from the throng, are even now laying their daily eggs for you at the back of the thickest bush. Your little dog rushes frantically up and down the front bed of your garden barking and racing, and tearing up the ground, because his rival little dog who lives down the street is going past with his master, and each pretends that he wants to be at the other — as they have pretended every day for the past three years. But the performance he goes through in the garden doesn't disturb you. Why should it? By following the directions in this article you have selected plants that he cannot hurt. After breakfasting at 12 noon, you stroll out, and, perhaps, smooth with your foot or with your small spade the inequalities made by the hens; you gather up casually the eggs that they have laid; you whistle to your little dog, and go out for a stroll with a light heart. That is the true way to enjoy amateur gardening.

# The Cat

F EW KNOW anything about domestic animals — about their inner life and the workings of their minds. Take, for instance, the common roof-tree cat. Most people think that the cat is an unintelligent animal, fond of ease, and caring little for anything but mice and milk. But a cat has really more character than most human beings, and gets a great deal more satisfaction out of life. Of all the animal kingdom, the cat has the most many-sided character. He — or she — is an athlete, a musician, an acrobat, a Lothario, a grim fighter, a sport of the first water. All day long, the cat loafs about the house and takes things easy, and sleeps by the fire, and allows himself to be pestered by the attentions of silly women and annoyed by children. To pass the time away he sometimes watches a mouse hole for an hour or two — just to keep himself from dying of ennui, and people get the idea that this sort of thing is all that life holds for the cat. But watch him as the shades of evening fall, and you see the cat as he really is.

When the family sits down to tea, the cat usually puts in an appearance to get his share, and he purrs noisily and rubs himself against the legs of the family, and all the time he is thinking of a fight or a love affair that is coming off that evening. If there is a guest at table the cat is particularly civil to him, because the guest is likely to have the best of what food is going. Sometimes, instead of recognising his civility with something to eat, the guest stoops down and strokes the cat, and says, "Poor pussy! Poor pussy!" The cat soon gets tired of that — he puts up his claw and quietly but firmly rakes the guest in the leg.

"Ow!" says the guest, "the cat stuck his claw into me!" The family is delighted. It remarks, "Isn't it sweet of him? Isn't he intelligent? *He wants you to give him something to eat.*"

The guest dare not do what he would like to do — kick the cat through the window — so with tears of rage and pain in his eyes, he affects to be very much amused, and sorts out a bit of fish from his plate and gives it to the cat. The cat gingerly receives it, with a look in his eyes as much as to say: "Another time, my friend, you won't be so dull of comprehension," and purrs maliciously as he carries the bit of fish away to a safe distance from the guest's boot before eating it. A cat isn't a fool — not by a long way.

When the family has finished tea, and gathers round the fire to enjoy the hours of indigestion together, the cat slouches casually out of the room and disappears. Life, true life, now begins for him. He saunters down his own backyard, springs to the top of the fence with one easy bound, drops lightly down the other side, trots across a right-of-way to a vacant allotment, and skips to the roof of an empty shed. As he goes, he throws off the effeminate look of civilisation; his gait becomes lithe and panther-like; he looks quickly, keenly, from side to side, and moves noiselessly, for he has many enemies — dogs, cabmen with whips, and small boys with stones. Arrived on the top of the shed, the cat arches his back and rakes his claws once or twice through the soft bark of the old roof, then wheels round and stretches himself a few times, just to see that every muscle is in full working order; and then, dropping his head nearly to his paws, sends across a league of backyards his call to his kindred — his call to love, or war, or sport.

Before long they come — gliding, graceful shadows, approaching circuitously, and halting occasionally to look round and reconnoitre — tortoiseshell, tabby, and black, all domestic cats, but all transformed for the nonce into their natural state. No longer are they the hypocritical, meek creatures who an hour ago were cadging for fish and milk. They are now ruffling, swaggering blades with a Gascon sense of their dignity. Their fights are grim, determined battles, and a cat will be clawed to ribbons before he'll yield. Even the young lady cats have this inestimable superiority over human beings that they can fight among themselves, and work off the jealousy, hatred and malice of their lives in a sprawling, yelling combat on a flat roof. All cats fight, and all keep themselves more or less in training while they are young. Your cat may be the acknowledged lightweight champion of his district — a Griffo of the feline ring! Just think how much more he gets out of his life than you do out of yours — what a hurricane of fighting and love-making his life is — and blush for yourself. You have had one little love affair, and never a good, all-out fight in your life!

And the sport they have, too! As they get older and retire from the ring they go in for sport more systematically, and the suburban backyards that are to us but dullness indescribable, are to them hunting grounds and trysting places where they may have more sport and adventure than ever had King Arthur's knights or Robin Hood's merry men. Grimalkin decides to go and kill a canary in a neighbouring verandah. Consider the fascination of it — the stealthy reconnaissance from the top of the fence; the care to avoid waking the house dog; the noiseless approach and the hurried dash upon the verandah, and the fierce clawing at the fluttering bird till the mangled body is dragged through the bars of the cage; the exultant retreat with the spoil and the growling over the feast that follows. Not the least entertaining part of it is the demure satisfaction of arriving home in time for breakfast and hearing the house-mistress say, "Tom must be sick; he seems to have no appetite."

It is always levelled as a reproach against cats that they are more fond of their home than of the people in it. Naturally, the cat doesn't like to leave his country, the land where he has got all his friends, and where he knows every landmark. Exiled in a strange land, he would have to learn a new geography, would have to find out all about another tribe of dogs, would have to fight and make love to an entirely new nation of cats. Life isn't long enough for that sort of thing and so, when the family moves, the cat, if allowed, will stay at the old house and attach himself to the new occupiers. He will give them the privilege of boarding him while he enjoys life in his own way. He is not going to sacrifice his whole career for the doubtful reward which fidelity to his old master or mistress might bring.

And if people know so little about cats, how much less do they know about the dog? This article was started as an essay on the dog, and the cat was only incidentally to be referred to, but there was so much to say about cats that they have used up all the space, and a fresh start must be made to deal with the dog — the friend of man.

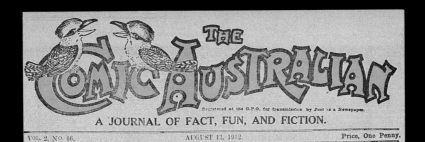

A JOURNAL OF FACT, FUN, AND FICTION.

VOL. 2, NO. 46.    AUGUST 13, 1912.    Price, One Penny.

"My, Sissie, you are a toff."

"Here, now, butcher, don't you get puttin' on dog "

"Dog, did you say? Where?"

!!? . . . !!??——!!

1. " My, Sissie, you are a toff. "
2. " Here, now butcher, don't you get puttin' on dog. "
3. " Dog, did you say? Where? "
4. ! ! ? ...! ! ? ? - ! !

# The Dog

THE CAT is the *roué*, sportsman, gambler, gay Lothario of the animal kingdom. The dog is the workman, a member of society who likes to have his day's work, and who does it more conscientiously than most human beings. A dog always looks as if he ought to have a pipe in his mouth and a black bag for his lunch, and then he would go quite happily to the office every day.

A dog without work is like a man without work, a nuisance to himself and everybody else. People who live about town, and keep a dog to give the children hydatids and to keep the neighbours awake at night, imagine that the animal is fulfilling his destiny and is not capable of anything better. All town dogs, fancy dogs, show dogs, lap-dogs, and dogs with no work to do should be at once abolished; it is only in the country that a dog has any justification for his existence.

The old theory that animals have only instinct and not reason is knocked endways by the dog. A dog can reason as well as a human being on some subjects, and better on others; and undoubtedly the best reasoning dog of all is the sheepdog. The sheepdog is a professional artist with a pride in his business. Watch any drover's dogs bringing sheep into the yards. How thoroughly they feel their responsibility, and how very annoyed they get if any stray vagrant dog with no occupation wants them to stop and fool about! They snap at him and hurry off as much as to say, "You go about your idleness. Don't you see this is my busy day?"

Dogs are followers of Carlyle. They hold that the only happiness for a dog in this life is to find his work and to do it. The idle, *dilettante*, non-working aristocratic dog they have no use for.

The training of a sheepdog for his profession begins at a very early age. The first thing is to take him out with his mother and let him see her working. He blunders out lightheartedly, frisking about in front of the horse, and he gets his first lesson that day, for his owner tries to ride over him, and generally succeeds. That teaches him one thing — to keep behind the horse till he is wanted. It is amusing to see how it knocks all the gas out of a puppy, and with what a humble air he falls to the rear and glues himself to the horse's heels, scarcely daring to look to the right or to the left for fear he may commit some other breach of etiquette. Then he watches the old slut work, and is allowed to go with her round the sheep, and, as likely as not, if he shows any disposition to get out of hand and frolic about, the old lady will bite him sharply to prevent his interfering with her work. Then by degrees, slowly, like any other professional, he learns his business. He learns to bring sheep after a horse simply at a wave of the hand; to force the mob up to a gate where they can be counted or drafted; to follow the scent of lost sheep and to drive sheep through a town without any master, one dog going on ahead to block the sheep from turning off into by-streets, while the other drives them on from the rear.

How do they learn all these things? Dogs for show work are taught painstakingly by men who are skilled in handling them, but after all they teach themselves more than the men teach them. There is no doubt that the acquired knowledge of generations is transmitted from dog to dog. The puppy, descended from a race of good sheepdogs, starts with all his faculties directed towards the working of sheep; he is half-educated as soon as he is born. He can no more help working sheep than a born musician can help playing the fiddle, or a Hebrew can help making money. It is bred in him. If he can't get sheep to work, he will work a fowl; often one can see a collie pup painstakingly and carefully driving a bewildered old hen into a stable or a stockyard, or any other enclosed space on which he has fixed his mind. How does he learn to do that? He didn't learn it at all. The knowledge was born with him.

It would be interesting to get examples of this inherited ability, and only that I don't want to let a flood of dog-liars loose on the paper, I would suggest to the editor to invite correspondence from those who have seen unquestionable examples of young, untaught animals doing things which they could only have learnt by inheritance.

When the dog has been educated, or educated himself, he enjoys his work; but sometimes, if he thinks he has had enough of it, he will deliberately quit and go home. Very few dogs like work "in the yards". The sun is hot, the dust rises in clouds, and there is nothing to do but bark, bark, bark, which is all very well for learners and amateurs but is beneath the dignity of the true professional sheepdog. Then, when the dogs are hoarse with barking and nearly choked with dust, the men lose their tempers and swear at them, and throw clods of earth at them, and sing out to them, "Speak up, blast you!" At last the dogs suddenly decide that they have done enough for the day, and, watching their opportunity, they silently steal over the fence, and go and hide in any cool place they can find. After a while the men notice that hardly any dogs are left, and then operations are suspended while a great hunt is made into all outlying pieces of cover, where the dogs are sure to be found lying low and looking as guilty as so many thieves. A clutch at the scruff of the neck, a kick in the ribs, and the dog is hauled out of his hiding place, and accompanies his master to the yard, frolicking about and pretending that he is quite delighted to be going back to work, and only happened to have hid in that bush out of sheer thoughtlessness. He is a champion hypocrite, is the dog.

After working another ten minutes, he will be over the fences again; and he won't hide in the same place twice. The second time he will be a lot harder to find than the first time.

Dogs, like horses, have very keen intuition. They know when a man is frightened of them, and they know when the men around them are frightened, though they may not know the cause. In the great Queensland strike, when the shearers attacked Dagworth shed, some rifle volleys were exchanged. The shed was burnt, and the air was full of human electricity, each man giving out waves of fear and excitement. Mark now the effect it had on the dogs. They were not in the fighting; nobody fired at them, and nobody spoke to them; but every dog left his master, left the sheep, and went away about six miles to the homestead. There wasn't a dog about the shed next day, after the fight. They knew there was something out of the common in the way of danger. The noise of the rifles would not frighten them, because many of them were dogs that were very fond of going out turkey shooting.

The same thing happened constantly with horses in the South African war. A loose horse would feed contentedly about while his own troops were firing; but when the troops were being fired at, and a bullet or two whistled past, the horses at once became uneasy, and the loose ones would trot away. The noise of a bullet passing cannot have been as terrifying to them as the sound of a rifle going off, but the nervousness and excitement of the men communicated itself to them. There are more capacities in horses and dogs, Horatio, than are dreamt of in your philosophy.

Dogs have an amazing sense of responsibility. Sometimes, when there are sheep to be worked, an old slut, who has young puppies, may be seen greatly exercised in her mind whether she should go out or not. On the one hand, she does not care about leaving the puppies; on the other, she feels that she really ought to go out, and not let the sheep be knocked about by those learners. Hesitatingly, with many a look behind her, she trots out after the horses and the other dogs. An impassioned appeal from the head boundary rider, "Go on back home, will yer!" is treated with the contempt it deserves. She goes out to the yards, works, perhaps half the day, and then slips quietly under the fences and trots off home, contented.

Besides the sheepdog there are hunting, sporting, and fighting dogs who all devote themselves to their professions with a diligence that might well be copied by human beings; there is no animal so thoroughly in earnest as a dog. But this article is long enough. Hunting, sporting and fighting dogs must be dealt with at another time; and, meanwhile, any readers who can forward any striking instances of canine sagacity should write same out in ink on one side of the paper only, get them attested by a missionary, mark them "Dog Story", and forward them to this office, where they will, as a rule, be carefully burnt.

# The Oracle in the Private Bar

"CUMANAVADRINK!" said the Thin Man to the Oracle, when they met at the corner hotel, and he moved to the main entrance.

"I never go into the threepenny bar," said the Oracle, "because I am liable to gout, and can't drink beer, and they can't sell anything drinkable for threepence but beer, which they ought to sell for twopence now that the brewers have reduced the wholesale price; but threepence seems to be what the Japanese in their weekly ultimatums to the Czar of Russia call the irreducible minimum."

"Well, come into the private bar," said the Thin Man.

And they did.

"Of course, you know why this is called the private bar?" said the Oracle.

"Well, no I don't," said the man of slight obesity.

"It is called the private bar," said the Oracle, "because it is open to the public. That is, it is open to those members of the public who are the happy possessors of the irreducible minimum of one sprat. To every possessor of sixpence a private bar is a public bar, and to every person with less than threepence a public bar is a private bar. In fact, he is barred altogether. In this country you cannot look at a barman through the end of a long-necked tumbler, or through the glass bottom of a pint pot, for less than threepence; that, as Admiral Kamimura would say, is the irreducible minimum."

"I see," said the Thin Man, who was so thin that his friends used to ask him if he were a grandson of Napoleon Boney Party.

"Hennessey and Schweppe, my dear," said the Oracle to the flaxen-haired Hebe behind the bar, "and my friend will have the same, because he knows that when you sell a fair nobbler of brandy and soda for sixpence you do so at a dead loss; while, if you sell two for a shilling and split the soda there is a profit of very nearly a halfpenny!"

"But I could come in and have a Hennessey and Schweppe on my own for sixpence, couldn't I?" inquired the Thin Man, well knowing that he could do so.

"Of course you could," said the Oracle.

"Then why, if it doesn't pay them, do they sell one brandy and soda for sixpence?"

"It's the quantity they sell that makes it pay," said the Oracle. "I am inclined to think," he went on, as he half emptied his glass, "that drink should be put down."

The barmaid smiled, and the Oracle frowned.

"This," he said, pointing to the young woman, "seems to be a very respectable girl; but I do not think a bar is a proper place for a girl. In this view I have the support of many estimable persons, who have never been inside an hotel, and consequently do not know anything at all about them. The number of things which are condemned by people who know nothing at all about them is one of the quaintest paradoxes of the twentieth century. Did you ever know a temperance lecturer to come into a bar, have a drink, shout for the barmaid, and invite her to Manly to shoot the chute and tobog the toboggan? No! Why? Because he is afraid it would be a Steyne on his character! But, as Antony said to Cleopatra, as recorded by the immortal bard, 'Let's to billiards!'"

"Who was the immortal bard?" asked the Thin Man.

"I refer," said the Oracle, "to William W. Shakespeare, the greatest of all English poets, and the first to mention the game of billiards. Apparently he played billiards, and probably Ben Jonson called him the Spot Stroke Bard."

"I observe," said the Oracle, when they reached the billiard room, and he was searching the rack for a cue with a tip as big as a shilling, "I observe that the Labour party have constructed an entirely new platform of six planks, all cut off their own heads, and I have no doubt that they have wood enough left to make another half-dozen. Shall I play you with a ten break, or give you fifty in a hundred?"

"Oh, we'd better play level," said the Thin Man.

"Play level!" cried the Oracle; "what's your name; Memmott?"

"No," said the Thin Man.

"Who'll break?" said the Oracle.

"I'll toss you for it," said the Thin Man.

"Oh, if we toss for it you probably won't have a shot at all. I can often make a hundred off the red from baulk. John Roberts used to pay me £200 a year to stop in Australia. He was afraid, you see, if I went to England I would be matched against him. Grand player, John. Did it ever strike you that the man who reaches the highest position in his trade or profession is generally named Roberts?"

"Nonsense!" said the Thin Man.

"No nonsense about it," went on the Oracle. "Look at John Roberts as a billiardist. Look at Lord Roberts as a general. Well, I'll break 'em up, give you 98 start, and bet you five bob you don't score at all."

"It's a wager," said the Thin Man, and the marker smiled as he put him on to 98.

Then the Oracle fired straight into the middle pocket and the game was over.

"You're out," said the Oracle, "and I'll have to pay for the table out of the five bob I won from you on the side wager that you wouldn't score!"

"I don't like this way of playing billiards," said the Thin Man.

"Oh, it's like Bill Scroggins," said the Oracle. "It's all right when you know it, but you've got to know it first. Have another game? No? All right. Let's have another drink."

They returned to the P.B. — the Private Bar, the Pretty Barmaid, and the Pale Brandy.

"Drink," repeated the Oracle, as he again emptied his glass, "drink should be put down."

"You seem to be putting it down all right," said the barmaid.

"And barmaids," went on the Oracle, "should also be put down. A beautiful creature like this leads men to drink. How much a week do you spend in drink?"

"Probably a pound," said the Thin Man.

"And how long have you been a drinker at that rate?"

"About twenty years."

"Ah, well, I was a teetotaller for forty years, that is what makes my hand so steady at billiards. You noticed my steady hand, probably, as I fired into that middle pocket? And you have been spending a pound a week in liquor for twenty years. Disgraceful! Twenty times fifty-two equals 1040. You have spent £1040 in drink, and probably kept sober all the time. Must have kept fairly sober, or you couldn't have earnt the money to buy liquor. Do you know, sir, that if you had put that pound per week into the Post Office Savings Bank, or into any other bank at a reasonable interest, you might now be the happy owner of a terrace of three or four fairly good houses?"

"Very likely," said the Thin Man. "Where's your terrace of houses?"

"Eh?" queried the Oracle.

"Where is your terrace of houses?"

"I've got no houses," said the Oracle.

"Well, where's the money?" asked the Thin Man.

"I'll tell you," said the Oracle, "if you promise not to let the matter go any further than the columns of a newspaper. The money that I didn't spend in drink during the forty years I was a teetotaller is in the same place as Mr Thomas Waddell's next surplus!"

# How I Shot the Policeman

HE WAS a short, fat, squat, bald-headed officer with a keen instinct for whisky, and an unlimited capacity for taking things "easy"; he would have been a tall man had Providence not turned round so much of his legs to make his feet. He used to "mooch" about the village at night, and if he saw any lights burning late in the houses, he would casually look in to see that nothing was amiss, and pretend to be very vigilant and on the alert, and he very often was rewarded with a stiff drink of whisky. If he had no excuse to go in, he used to rattle at the gates to see that the fastenings were all right, and when the proprietor came out he would say, "All right, sir! I was just seeing that the gate was fast! Very dry night, sir!" And this generally ended in a liquid and spirituous manner. But the system one night resulted in serious damage to the constable himself, as I shall proceed to explain.

I was reading for an examination and burning the midnight oil; in front of the house was a small garden, into which an old grey horse that belonged to an Irishman up the village was constantly straying down the road and making his way. He could lift the gate catch with his nose, and many a time in the stilly night I used to hear him rattling at it trying to get the gate open. Then I would leave my books, and sally out and drive him away with language and blue metal. Next time he happened to be loose he would play the same game. He became very crafty too, and would clear out like lightning the moment he heard anyone stirring in the house, so that it became a most difficult matter to land a rock on him at all. Tired of this kind of thing, I one night prepared a little surprise for him. I got a two-pound dumb-bell, laid it ready in the balcony overlooking the gate, so that I could rush out and get it the moment I heard him: and I calculated to give him the hardest knock he ever had. Then I went back to the books and read on.

The night wore on and midnight approached: it was dark as the inside of a cow, and a little wind was blowing. Suddenly I heard a faint "rattle, rattle" down at the gate. I drew a long breath, slipped noise lessly into the balcony, grasped the dumb-bell and let it go with terrific force right at a dim object just looming through the pitchy darkness.

The astute reader will, of course, have divined that it was not the old grey horse this time. It was the policeman. The two-pound iron dumb-bell had struck him fair on the temple; if it had hit him anywhere else it would have killed him.

He threw up his hands and fell like a dead man. I rushed to his assistance. It is useless to try and set out half the things that flashed through my brain as I rushed downstairs. In my mind's eye I saw myself before the coroner's jury; I saw myself at the criminal court with Judge Windeyer trying me; I heard the jury bring in a verdict of guilty with a strong recommendation to mercy, and I knew *that* meant hanging for certain, as people recommended to mercy always perish on the scaffold in Australia. I saw a blotched diagram of the locality published in the daily papers with a cross to mark the spot where the policeman fell, and an asterisk to show the position of the murderer when he hurled the bloodthirsty dumb-bell. I saw my portrait — that of a dreadful-looking ruffian — in the *Town and Country Journal* — and then, having reached the prostrate form of the blue-bottle, I lifted him in my arms and ascertained that he still lived. With tender care I bathed his alabaster brow; I watched with eagerness as he slowly came round; as soon as he was conscious I began to apologise, to explain, to grovel. He listened for a while and then he said, "Oh, it's all right, Banjo. It was an unfortnit haccident. Do you happen to have a little whisky in the house? My tongue is dry enough to strike matches on."

I loaded him up with whisky, gave him a substantial Christmas box and sent him on his way as good as new. I believe you could shoot him with dumb-bells every night in the week on the same terms.

# The
# Tug-of-War

THE FIRST night of the Tug-of-War at Darlinghurst Hall, Sydney, was a great affair. There was a big crowd, mostly Irishmen and what are called "foreigners". The tugs took place on a long narrow platform, having stout battens nailed across it; the men laid their feet against these battens and lay right down to their pull. It was a straight-out test of strength and endurance; but it was whispered about the hall that the Irishmen and the West Indian darkies had not room for their feet between the battens. This should be seen to. There was a parading of teams for a start, and a very fine-looking lot of men they were. Then the Italians came out to pull the Norwegians. The Italian team were mostly fishermen; their rivals were sailors and wharf labourers. It looked any odds on the Norsemen, who were a long way the heavier team, and they won the pull. But the children of Garibaldi fought firmly for every inch, and stuck to it for half and hour. It was a desperate struggle. The crowd were very facetious, and yelled much good advice to the fair-haired men — "Now boys, don't let the ice-cream push beat you," "Pull the organ-grinders over," "Go it, Macaroni," — and so forth. An interval for drinks — here, the referee took a drink — and the Denmark team had a walk-over, the Welshmen having scratched. The Taffies had not time to get a team together. Then another walk-over, France failing to appear against Sweden. The frog-eaters rely mainly on style and deportment in everything they do, and there are no points given for style in tug-of-war!

Then came what was supposed to be the tug of the evening, Australia *v* Ireland. As the teams took their places, you could feel the electricity rising in the atmosphere. The Irish were a splendid team, a stone a man heavier than their opponents all round, but the latter looked, if anything, harder and closer-knit. As they took their places the warning bells rang out all over the building: "Now, boys, Sunny N.S.W., for it!" "Go it, Australia!" And from the Irish side came a babel of broad, soft, buttery brogue: "Git some chark on yer hands, Dinny," "Mick, if yez don't win, niver come back to the wharf no more," "For the love o' God and my fiver, bhoys, pull together!" It was a national Irish team right through — regular Donegal and Tipperary bhoys. The Swedes might have been Swedes from Surry Hills, the Russians might have first seen the light at Cockatoo Island, but there was no gammon about the Irish. They were genuine; every other man answered to the name of Mike. They wore orange and green colours, to give the Pope and the Protestants an equal show. Then they spat on their enormous hands, planted their brogues against the battens, and at the the sound of the pistol, while every Australian's heart beat high with hope, the Mickies simply gave one enormous dray horse drag and fetched our countrymen clean away hand over hand, pulling them about ten feet more than was necessary before they could be stopped. How did their supporters cheer! Ahoo! Ahoo! The building rang again with wild shouts of exultation. It was a great day for Donegal entirely, likewise for Cork and Killarney. The Australians present pulled their hats down over their eyes and looked at their toes. One man wanted to back a team of lightweight jockeys to pull anything anybody would fetch, but this pleasantry could not avert the sting of defeat. There was no disguising it — the Australians were "beat bad", and the glory of Woolloomooloo had departed.

Next came the West Indies versus Maoriland, which was a very funny business. The Maorilanders were small and weedy compared to their sable opponents, but they hung on gamely. The coloured gentlemen, as seen from the M.L. end, presented a most remarkable sight. Firstly the eye caught the soles of their huge, flat feet, sticking up in the air like so many shovels; their feet hid their bodies altogether, and only allowed their heads to be seen. The heads were all as round as apples, black as ink, and each one had in it two white dots — the glaring eyeballs of the owner. As these remarkable people swayed in unison behind the ramparts of their feet, they looked like — well, it's no good trying to say what they looked like. There is nothing in heaven above, or the earth beneath, or the water under the earth, that will furnish the feeblest comparison. They pulled like good 'uns, and amid loud yells of, "Go it, Snowball!" the Maorilanders were pulled over, fighting hard to the last.

Then "Rule Britannia" from the band, and the English team marched on to the platform — all very neatly dressed, neatly shaven, moving with great precision. "What are they at all?" "A team of marines from the men-of-war." They *looked* fit to pull a house down. Then the squawk of the band changed to "The Watch on the Rhine", and the sons of the Fatherland came up to do or die for the country of sauerkraut. It looked any odds on the English. But they were white-skinned and flaccid, while the deep, sunburnt hue of the other arms told of hard, toughening work. Bang went the pistol, and after a terrible tussle the Rhinelanders fairly wore out the Britishers and scored a gallant win. There was a strong British section present, and their disappointment was intense. A man-o'-war's man was with difficulty stopped from climbing onto the platform and offering to pull the heads off the whole blanky Dutch team. This win was a surprise, but a bigger surprise was in store when the Russians met the Scotch. Where they found a team of ten Russians in Sydney goodness only knows, but they were gaunt, wiry, hard-featured men — some of them obviously Russian Finns, than whom the earth produces no stronger or more resolute race. Their opponents had a smug, comfortable look, and seemed a long way the stouter men. The Russians were all seamen and seafaring men of some sort. At the signal to go, the Russians gained a little, and then began a tremendous wavering pull, each side alternately gaining and losing. The Scotch supporters cheered their men on with wild cries. The Australians impartially barracked both sides. First they would give the Scotch a turn — "Go it, Donald!" "Haul away Sandy!" "Go it, Burgoo!" Then they would turn their attention to the Russians: "Go it, Siberia!" "We'll have to get the knout to you fellows," and so on. But all the foreign nations seemed to form a sort of Mafia to encourage the Russians against the Scotch. Norseman, Dane, and Dago joined in the wild chorus of encouragement. An old man, apparently the father of one of the Russian team, danced alongside the platform shrieking in every language under the sun. The man he was cheering was a great broad-chested giant who threw his mighty strength on to the rope in tremendous surges, and at every pull the old man would howl — "Go on, Manuel, you're doing splendid." Then he would sing out something like "Kyohjnoo," and Manuel would give another heave that would fetch the Scotch team another two or three inches at least. He was a magnificent man, was Manuel. The great wiry muscles stood out on his arms like knotted ropes. And when at last it only wanted six inches more for a win, Manuel lifted his head and gave the old sailor-cry that the men of the sea know so well and respond to — "Yo, heave-ho-o-o-o-o," and the subjects of the Great White Czar gave one mighty lift that fetched the Scotchmen away as if they had been children. It was a grand pull, and one's sympathies went with the little band of Russians, because if they are really Russians (their faces seemed Slavonic) there must have been very few men to pick from, whereas here every third man is a Scotchman. It will be seen, therefore, that the Germans beat the English, the Russians beat the Scotch, and the West Indian blacks beat the Maorilanders. Perhaps (whisper it softly) — perhaps the British and the Australians are not the only strong and determined races on the face of the earth after all.

The Irish on the first night certainly looked like winning. It is said that the team has been carefully picked — that scores of men were tried and rejected before the team was formed. The Continental nations have very few men to choose from. The Australians ought to go and practise pulling the hair off a pound of butter before they compete. They may do better later on. We intend to be there again for a good long evening when the black men meet the Irish. And if you want to get your two eyes knocked straight into one, go and "barrack" against the land of Erin.

In Australia, however, nothing is complete without a strike, and on Monday the teams mostly struck. They wanted a total sum of £156 a night, and the management didn't see it. Then the Italian gentlemen, full of a desire to recover their lost glory, offered to throw themselves into the gap, and were set down as "scabs". By and by a compromise was arrived at, and the show began forty-five minutes late. Scotland and Norway took the rope and in six minutes the former went under amid the ruins of the thistle and the haggis, while a spectral voice in kilts groaned over their discomfiture. Russia, with the potent Manuel on deck, broke Germany up in about twelve minutes, and the signs, at time of writing, seem to be that the sons of the Great White Czar will come out on top. Manuel — we are not quite sure that his name *is* Manuel, but it doesn't matter — is an awful snag to strike, especially when his aged father barracks for him and urges him on. The longest pull of the evening was between the Englishmen and the West Indies darkies, and here for the first time the Anglo-Saxon race got a show. It took them over an hour to do it, but at the end of that time Ham went under. He deserved better luck, did Ham, especially as he is the lightest team in the show. Australia again had the distinction of knocking under in shorter time than anybody else; he was a disgraced kangaroo in just thirty-three seconds, the Maorilanders bolting with him as if they intended to rush down to Circular Quay. Ireland also went under to Sweden, which was a painful surprise to many individuals named Mick, Terence, and Dinny. Last of all, Italy came on to give a mighty heave for the honour of the banana-vending industry. Denmark took the other end of the rope and held it for thirty-three minutes, and then the stupendous efforts of the fallen Romans carried the day. France and Wales both failed to turn up.

After Monday night's proceedings, Norway, Sweden and Russia were ahead with two wins each, and Ireland, West Indies, Italy, England, Denmark, Germany and Maoriland had one apiece. France and Wales have been on strike since the start, and Scotland and Australia come in dejectedly at the tail with two blanks. If Manuel's boiler doesn't burst, or his father doesn't break a blood vessel while howling for him, Russia should win the big prize; and Italy, if only on account of the demoniac energy of the hulking gentleman with the large feet who pulls at the extreme end of the rope, should be close up. The *Bulletin* suggests that that huge Roman and Manuel should pull each other single-handed at the close of proceedings. It would be a gaudy spectacle. The Roman's name, we believe, is Julius Caesar.

# My
# *Various Schools*

I N WRITING about schools which I have at different periods attended, I will pass over my infantile experience of an old dame's school in a suburb of Sydney; also of a small public school to which I crept unwillingly, like a snail, for a few months. I pass these over because I don't remember much about them, and what little I do remember is unpleasant.

The first school which I attended in the capacity of a reasoning human creature was a public school in a tired little township away out in the bush, at the back of the Never Never, if you know where that is. I lived on a station four miles from the school, and had to go up paddock every morning on foot, catch my pony, and ride him down to the house barebacked, get breakfast, ride the four miles, and be in school by half-past nine o'clock. Many a time in the warm summer mornings have I seen the wonderful glories of a bush sunrise, when comes

> The still silent change,
> When all fire-flushed the forest trees redden
> On slopes of the range,
> When the gnarl'd, knotted trunks Eucalyptian
> Seem carved, like weird columns Egyptian,
> With curious device, quaint inscription,
> And hieroglyph strange.

I think Australian boys who have never been at school in the bush have lost something for which town life can never compensate. However, let me get on to the school, where I mingled with the bush youngsters who, from huts and selections and homesteads far and near, had gathered there. They were a curious lot. Perhaps their most striking characteristic was their absolute want of originality. They had one standard excuse whenever they were late: "Father sent me after 'orses." They didn't garnish it with a "Sir", or anything of the sort, but day after day every boy that was late handed in the same unvarnished statement, and took his caning as a matter of course. As their parents were largely engaged in looking after horses, mostly others people's, it had colour of probability at first, but after a time it wore out and they were too lazy or too stupid to invent anything to replace it. I thought I could mend this state of things, having a particularly vigorous and cultivated imagination, so one day, when a lot were late, I supplied each of them with a different excuse. One was to have forgotten his book and gone back for it, another was to have been misled as to the time by the sun getting up unusually late (not one in fifty had a clock in their house), another was to have been sent on an errand to the storekeeper's and been delayed by the clerk, and so forth. I was privileged and licensed to be late myself, having so far to come, so I simply walked in hurriedly as though I had done my best to arrive early and went to my seat. Then came the first of my confederates. "What makes you late, Ryan?" Ryan gasped, his eyes rolled, his jaw dropped, and then out it came, the old familiar formula — "Father sent me after 'orses." It was second nature to the boy. And all the others, one by one, as they faced the music, brought out the same old story, and took two cuts of the cane on each hand as per usual. I gave them up after that; my inventive talent was wasted upon such people.

The visit of the inspector used to be a great event in the school. Theoretically the inspector was supposed to come unheralded, and to drop on the master promiscuous-like, and so catch the school unprepared; but practically, when the inspector was in the town, the master always had a boy stationed on the fence to give warning of his approach, and by the time the inspector had toiled up the long hill to the school, that boy was back in his seat and every youngster was studying for dear life; and when the inspector asked us questions in arithmetic, the master used to walk absent-mindedly behind him and hold up his fingers to indicate the correct answer. Oh, he was a nice pedagogue!

In writing of a school, one ought to say something about the lessons, but I remember absolutely nothing of the curriculum, except the "handers" which formed, for the boys at any rate, the one absorbing interest of each day.

"Handers" were blows on the palm of the hand, administered with a stout cane. They were dealt out on a regular scale, according to the offence; not being able to answer a question, one on each hand; late at school, two on each hand; telling lies, three on each hand, etc., etc. The school was in a very cold climate, and perhaps the "handers" didn't sting at all on a cold frosty morning! Oh no, not in the least. We used to have wild theories that if you put resin on the palm of your hand the cane would split into a thousand pieces and cut the master's hand severely, but none of us had ever seen resin, so one's dreams of revenge were never realised. Sometimes fierce, snorting old Irishwomen used to come to the school and give the master some first-class Billingsgate for having laid on the "handers" too forcibly or too frequently on the hardened palm of her particular Patsy or Denny. We used to sit with open mouths and bulging eyes, while the dreaded pedagogue cowered before the shrill and fluent abuse of these ladies. They always had the last word, in fact the last hundred or more words, as their threats and taunts used to be distinctly audible as they faded away down the dusty hill.

When the railway came to the town, the children of the navvies came to the school, and how they did wake it up! Sharp, cunning little imps, they had travelled and shifted about all over the colony, they had devices for getting out of "handers" such as we had never dreamt of, they had a fluency in excuse and a fertility in falsehood which we could admire but never emulate. Sometimes their parents the navvies used to go on prolonged drinking bouts, and contract a disease, known to science, I believe, as "delirium tremens", but in our vocabulary as "the horrors" or "the jumps". The townsfolk shortened up even this brief nomenclature — they used simply to say that so-and-so "had 'em" or "had got 'em". Well do I remember the policeman, a little spitfire of a man about five feet nothing, coming to the school and stating that a huge navvy named Cornish Jack had "got 'em", and was wandering about the town with them, and he called upon the schoolmaster in the Queen's name to come and assist him to arrest "Cornish Jack". The teacher did not like the job at all, and his wife abused the policeman heartily, but it ended in the whole school going, and we marched through the town till we discovered the quarry seated on a log, pawing the air with his hands. The sergeant and the teacher surrounded him, so to speak, but to our disgust he submitted very quietly and was bundled into a cart and driven off to the lock-up. Such incidents as these formed breaks in the monotony of school life and helped to enlarge our knowledge of human nature.

There was not wanting some occasional element of sadness too. I remember one day all the boys were playing at the foot of a long hill covered with fallen timber; it was after school hours and one of the boys was given a bridle by his father and told to catch a horse that was feeding in hobbles on the top of the hill and bring him down. The boy departed, nothing loath, and caught the animal, a young half-broken colt, and boy-like mounted him barebacked and started to ride him down. The colt ran away with him and came sweeping down the hill at a racing pace, jumping fallen logs and stones, and getting faster and faster every moment. The boy rode him well, but at length he raced straight at a huge log, and suddenly, instead of jumping it, swerved off, throwing the boy with terrific force among the big limbs. His head was crushed in and he was dead before we got up to him. His people were Irish folk and the intense, bitter sadness of their grief was something terrible.

I left the bush school soon after that, and went to a private school in the suburbs of Sydney: a nice quiet institution where we were all young gentlemen, and had to wear good clothes instead of hobnailed boots and moleskins in which my late schoolmates invariably appeared. Also we were ruled by moral suasion instead of "handers"; a thing that I appreciated highly.

Very little of interest occurred there; a sickening round of lessons and washing. Nobody ever "had 'em", nobody was ever sent after horses; nobody wore spurs in school; most of the boys learnt dancing and some could play the piano. Let us draw a veil over it, and hurry on to the grammar school. But I think the Editor would have to get out an enlarged edition of the *Sydneian** if I opened the floodgates of my memory about the grammar school, so for the present, farewell.

**The Sydneian*  The magazine of Sydney Grammar School, College Street, Sydney.